Punishment of a Vixen

Barbara Cartland

Punishment of a Vixen

DURON BOOKS

Punishment of a Vixen

A Duron Book / July 1977

ISBN 0-87272-071-3

Duron Books are published by Brodart, Inc. Its trademark, consisting of
the words "Duron Books" is registered in the United States Patent Office and
in other countries.

PRINTED IN THE UNITED STATES OF AMERICA

Punishment of a Vixen

Chapter One

1903

The open carriage drawn by two horses stopped outside the door of the Villa and a gentleman got out.

As he paid the driver who had brought him from Cannes Station, he heard the sound of music coming from the house and saw that the garden was decorated with Chinese lanterns.

There was only one leather case to be set down and a footman running down the steps lifted it up to carry it into the house.

The driver touched his cap in acknowledgement of a generous tip.

As he drove away the gentleman stood for a moment on the steps looking between the tall dark cypress trees to where some distance away the Mediterranean gleamed in the moonlight.

It was very beautiful and the music in the background enhanced the inevitable suggestion of romance. Then he turned and walked up the steps to where in the hall the Butler was waiting for him.

"Good-evening, Mr. Tyrone," he said with the welcoming smile of an old retainer. "We were expecting you yesterday, Sir."

"Yes, I know, Ronaldson," the newcomer said, "but the trains from the East are invariably unpunctual and I arrived in Paris too late to catch my connection."

"Her Ladyship'll be very glad to hear you've arrived safely."

"Do not tell her until I have washed and changed," Tyrone Strome said. "I see you are having a party."

"Yes, Mr. Tyrone, a dinner-dance for the young people."

There was something almost contemptuous in the Butler's voice which made Tyrone Strome laugh.

He was well aware that Ronaldson, who had been with his sister's family for many years, disliked what he considered "informal occasions."

"Show me where I am to sleep," he suggested. "As I am travelling light, I doubt if I shall be smart enough for a party."

"Knowing, Sir, you'd doubtless be staying with Her Ladyship," Ronaldson answered, "I brought a suit of your evening-clothes with me from London."

Tyrone Strome smiled.

"I am grateful, Ronaldson, as I always am for the excellent way in which you look after me. I only wish I could take you with me on my travels."

"Heaven forbid, Mr. Tyrone!" the Butler exclaimed. "I would have enjoyed your type of life, Sir, when I was young, but I'm past adventuring at my age."

Tyrone Strome laughed quietly and followed Ronaldson as he moved slowly and rather pompously along a corridor on the ground floor of the Villa, passing a number of Salons as he did so.

He was aware that he would be sleeping in the rooms which he invariably occupied when he enjoyed his sister's hospitality.

He was however always so vague as to when he would arrive or when he would leave that he did not count on having special treatment, except that Ronaldson would have been affronted if he had not been accommodated in what the Butler considered proper style.

The rooms they finally reached were built out from the Villa, connected to it by a long covered passage.

The previous owner had been a writer who desired solitude and had therefore built himself what was to all intents and purposes a tiny chalet.

On the edge of a ravine, it had in the day-time a breath-taking view over the sea and coast.

High up on the hill, Lady Merrill's Villa had unequalled position, but even better than the main building itself was this small chalet which her brother always looked upon as his own.

"Everything is ready for you, Mr. Tyrone," the Butler said with satisfaction, "and I'll send a footman, Sir, to unpack your valise. He's French, but well up in his duties."

"Thank you, Ronaldson. As you realise, I have been travelling very light, but my yacht should be in harbour, in which case I have a number of things aboard which I can send for tomorrow."

"I think, Sir, you'll find everything you need this evening."

"I am sure I shall."

As he spoke Tyrone Strome climbed the narrow stairway from the Sitting-Room to the bed-room over it.

As he entered the attractive room in which the decorations were predominantly white, he saw his tail-coat and stiff shirt lying ready for him on a chair.

He looked at them and made a grimace, thinking how uncomfortable they would be after the casual clothes he had been wearing the last three months.

He had in fact been on a secret and at times dangerous mission to the East, travelling incognito; the passport he carried did not bear his real name.

When he had sent off his report from Paris last night, having in fact on arrival spent most of the night preparing it, he had known that certain people in London would be extremely pleased at what he had been able to achieve.

Tyrone Strome had always been a mystery man

to his contemporaries, to his friends, and even to his sister, who adored him.

He had worked in the Foreign Office for some years. Then unexpectedly and without explanation he had taken to travelling to obscure parts of the world, leaving no address behind and being very reluctant on his return to talk of where he had been.

Many people considered him just an inveterate traveller. It was only in a certain anonymous department of the Foreign Office that Tyrone Strome's name was always spoken of with awe and respect.

Now, when he knew he could relax the pressure under which he had worked for the last months, he felt suddenly very tired.

It was, he knew, the reaction to having to be permanently on the alert and on his guard; never being able to enter a room without thinking that some-one might be behind the door; never being able to speak without choosing every word with care.

Now it was all over, he thought, and he intended to enjoy himself with his sister Helene and make no plans for the future until they were forced upon him.

He started to undress and as he did so there was a knock at the door and the footman Ronaldson had sent entered.

"I've come to unpack, *Monsieur*," he said in French.

"Thank you," Tyrone Strome said. "There is only my valise."

He pointed to where the other footman had left it beside the wardrobe, then throwing his coat onto a chair walked into the bath-room.

One of the pleasant things about his sister's Villa was that it had modern bath-rooms of a type that were rare in Europe.

The Americans, Tyrone Strome thought, were al-most like the Ancient Romans in their desire to bathe frequently, and they made sure there were a number of luxurious bath-rooms in every house they occupied.

In Europe, especially in England, the choice was usually between a hip-bath in one's bed-room with

brass cans of water dragged up innumerable stairs by
sweating servants, or a bath-room situated at the end
of a long, cold corridor where it took hours for the hot
tap to produce anything but tepid water.

Lying in the deep, warm, comfortable bath with
which he was provided here in the South of France,
Tyrone felt as if he washed away not only the dust of
his journey but also the anxieties which had made his
latest exploit a hair-raising experience.

It had been one of the most difficult assignments
he had ever undertaken, and he told himself that his
success entitled him to have a very long and lazy
holiday.

This he intended to spend with his sister, who
was the only close member of his family alive and for
whom he had an unswerving devotion.

Lady Merrill was in fact fourteen years older than
her brother and had mothered him after their mother
died when Tyrone was a very small boy.

Left a widow three years ago, she had only one
son, David, now Lord Merrill, whom she adored.

David had been at Oxford when Tyrone Strome
had last been with his sister and he remembered
now that he had not seen the boy for nearly two
years.

He looked forward to renewing his acquaintance
with his nephew, but he realised that as David was
now twenty-one he would not find the Villa as quiet
as it had been in the past.

There would be dinner-dances, of which Ronaldson obviously disapproved, doubtless taking place
night after night, and he told himself in that case he
would either stay quietly in his own chalet reading or
sleep aboard his yacht.

He had no intention of being part of the gay, glittering set which had made the Riviera one of the most
fashionable parts of Europe.

Monte Carlo had always drawn the famous and
the infamous ever since it had opened its doors to
gamblers, but the King when he was Prince of Wales
had made Cannes fashionable.

Now rich noblemen, politicians, and social-climb-ers were all seeking Villas in the vicinity.

"I have every intention of being quiet," Tyrone Strome told himself.

He knew he could rely on his sister not to try to lionise him as so many other people had tried to do.

It was not difficult to realise why.

Tyrone Strome was not only an interesting and wealthy young man who came from a distinguished family; he was also extremely handsome and had a mysterious, intriguing quality about him which women found irresistible.

They had no idea, of course, of the dangerous work in which he was so often engaged.

But no-one could have achieved what Tyrone Strome had in the past few years and not developed a personality which made him an object of interest and curiosity wherever he appeared.

As he dried himself now after his bath, an impar-tial observer would have thought that with his lean, athletic frame he looked like a Greek god.

He was outstandingly fit and when he went into his bed-room the French valet who was waiting to help him into his evening-clothes stared at him in admiration.

Tyrone Strome talked to the man in perfect French. Then when he was ready with the exception of his evening-coat he dismissed him.

"There is no need to wait."

"I will tidy up later, *Monsieur*."

"Thank you."

Tyrone Strome, waiting until the footman had withdrawn, turned out the lights and walked across the bed-room and through the open windows onto the balcony.

He wished to look at the beauty that lay beneath him and at the star-strewn sky.

He felt as if the loveliness of it soothed him, al-most like a cool hand on his forehead.

There was the smell of syringa and mimosa on the air, and he knew that the purple bougainvillaea and the pink, scented geraniums climbing over the balcony would in the morning hum with the sound of bees.

It was all very familiar and peaceful, and as he put his elbows on the balcony and felt a very faint breath of wind from the sea he wondered if he should stay here, content with his thoughts, and not join the party.

He felt out of tune with the noise and exuberance of young people, a dance-band, and the "pop" of champagne corks.

Then he told himself that the change was just what he needed.

He had been concentrating so fiercely on the problems and difficulties of his assignment that it would take some time for his brain to become less active, his senses less perceptive.

He was just about to take one last look to where the sea gleaming silver in the moonlight met the hazy horizon, when he heard voices below him.

"Listen to me, Nevada, I beg you! You have to listen!"

It was a man's voice and there was a note of urgency and pleading in it which seemed to Tyrone Strome to be almost like a signal of distress.

"There is no such word as 'must' where I am concerned," a woman replied.

"You have been avoiding me, Nevada, and it is driving me mad! Why have you changed? Why are you treating me like this?"

"Like what?"

The words were almost a drawl and Tyrone Strome thought that she had a touch of an accent.

"You know quite well what I mean. You were so kind and so sweet to me, then suddenly after sweeping me up to the highest heavens you dropped me down into the deepest hell!"

"Oh, David, how poetic!"

"Damnit, will you take seriously what I am saying? I love you, Nevada, and you are driving me insane!"

The woman gave a little laugh.

"How theatrical you are, and why do men always say the same things? I find your vocabulary very limited."

"You are mocking me, you are trying to make me more unhappy than I am already. How can you be so cruel—so unkind?"

Again the woman laughed.

"Complaints . . . always complaints! I cannot think why men are never satisfied."

"Do not keep on talking about men," David said savagely.

Tyrone Strome knew now that it was his nephew, David Merrill, who was speaking.

"I am not concerned with what you think about other men, but what you feel about me. I love you, Nevada. I want you to marry me. I have asked you often enough, and if you continue to laugh at me and hold me up as a figure of fun I shall do something desperate!"

"You are play-acting, David. You really would make your fortune on the stage! And what would this desperate act be? I am curious."

There was silence for a moment. Then David Merrill said solemnly:

"If you want to know the truth, I have considered shooting myself."

His companion went into a peal of laughter.

"How banal! I thought at least you would think of something original! Shooting one's self is what all my love-lorn swains threaten, but they never do it!"

"One day you will get a shock."

"Not a shock . . . a surprise! It might be quite interesting to see a dead body . . . I have never seen one."

"Nevada! Will you not talk like that? I love you! How often must I tell you so? I love you desperately! I cannot get you out of my thoughts or out of my mind. I cannot sleep for thinking of you. Say you will marry me! I swear I will make you happy."

"If you want the truth, I think you would make

me very unhappy," Nevada replied. "Quite frankly, David, I have no intention of saddling myself with a husband who is nothing but a hysterical boy."

"I am a man, and if you talk to me like that I will show you just how much of a man I am."

He made a movement towards her.

"Do not dare to touch me!"

The words were almost a snarl and she continued:

"You know I will not let anyone touch me. In fact I despise you because the love you offer me is not worth having!"

"What do you mean by that?" David asked.

"You are weak and brainless, or else you would find something better to do with your life than trying to end it. If I ever marry, which is most unlikely, let me tell you it will be with a man who can stand on his own two feet . . . a man who will take what he wants of life and not collapse at every set-back."

"You think that is what I am doing?" David Merrill asked savagely.

"I think you are young, inexperienced . . . and a bore!"

"But I love you!"

"It is the sort of love for which I have no use."

"You seemed fond enough of me once."

"That was before I knew you well. Have you ever asked yourself what you have to offer a woman . . . besides your title of course?"

There was no doubt that Nevada meant to be nasty.

"If that is what you feel about me then there is nothing more to be said," David answered.

"Nothing," Nevada agreed, "and so in the future leave me alone. Find someone else to whine to. Some women like yapping lap-dogs."

She walked away as she spoke and Tyrone Strome listening from the balcony heard the sound of her high heels on the paved path.

He leaned a little farther over the balcony and now he could see his nephew standing below him, his face silhouetted against the darkness of a cypress tree.

He was staring out to sea apparently in despair. Then, as he watched, Tyrone Strome saw him take something from his pocket.

With the instinct of a man who senses danger he moved quickly, put his leg over the balcony, let himself down by his arms, and dropped to the ground.

When he reached his nephew, David Merrill was staring at him in astonishment and holding a revolver in his hand.

Tyrone Strome walked towards him.

"Hello, David," he said. "I seem to have arrived at a somewhat inopportune moment."

"Uncle Tyrone!" David managed to exclaim.

"In person!" Tyrone Strome replied lightly.

Reaching out, he took the revolver from his nephew's hand and slipped it into the pocket of his trousers.

"I am afraid I could not help eavesdropping," he said quietly, "but to have announced my presence might have proved embarrassing."

David Merrill sat down on a garden-chair and put his head in his hands.

"What am I to do, Uncle Tyrone?" he asked. "She is driving me mad!"

"So I gathered."

Tyrone Strome took a chair near his nephew's and after a moment he said:

"You do not want to listen to the usual platitudes, and I have no intention of uttering them. Shall I instead suggest an alternative to staying here and being unhappy?"

"What else can I do?" David Merrill asked miserably. "She seemed to like me at first, then suddenly found every other man more interesting than me. I love her, and I can think of nothing else. If she will not marry me I might just as well be dead!"

"I said I had an alternative suggestion. Would you listen to it?"

"I suppose so."

David's tone was ungracious.

"I was in Paris last night," Tyrone Strome said. "When I arrived at the Ritz I found three friends I have known for a long time who were just going off to Africa on a big-game safari. They asked me to join them, as there had originally been four in the party, but someone had dropped out."

He realised that his nephew was attending as he went on:

"They intend not only to shoot, but also to explore parts of Central Africa about which very little is known."

He paused before he went on:

"Of course I realise that sort of thing may not interest you, but I promise you my friends are extremely charming, good shots, and experienced travellers."

"Are you suggesting that I should go with them?" David asked in a dull voice.

"Why not?" Tyrone Strome asked. "The alternative is of course to stay here and make yourself more miserable by trying to persuade a woman who obviously has no interest in you to change her mind. Something I think you know in your heart she is unlikely to do."

What he had heard of the conversation made Tyrone Strome think that Nevada, whoever she might be, was a most unpleasant young woman whom his nephew would do well to avoid.

But he was far too tactful and too sensitive to other people's feelings to say anything disparaging about the object of David's affections.

"Do you think that if I went with your friends Nevada would miss me?" David asked after a moment.

"I think all women miss an admirer when he is no longer there," Tyrone Strome said cautiously, "and I think, too, David, you would find your outlook on life would, after a journey of that sort, alter considerably."

"You are trying to say I should forget Nevada.

That is something which will not happen," David said sharply.

"I was not suggesting anything of the sort," his uncle replied. "What I was thinking was that you would become a much more interesting person. It is a cliché to say that travel broadens the mind, because it depends very much on the sort of travelling you do, but I can assure you Africa is a place of hidden possibilities and as-yet-undiscovered knowledge."

"I know that," David murmured.

"It would not interest you, of course," Tyrone Strome continued, "but the National Geographical Society consider that men who make that sort of journey are not only pioneers but heroes!"

"If I went," David said, almost as if he spoke to himself, "Nevada would realise I am not as gutless as she thinks."

There was a silence and after a moment Tyrone Strome said:

"There is only one difficulty."

"What is that?"

"You would have to leave tomorrow! I could wire my friends you are coming, but I am sure I am not mistaken in thinking that the ship in which they are sailing from Marseilles will leave late tomorrow night."

There was silence, a long silence, before David said loudly:

"I will go! Damnit, Uncle Tyrone, I will go! That will show Nevada, if nothing else, that I am not there only to be played with."

"I am sure you have made a wise choice, David," Tyrone Strome said.

His nephew jumped to his feet.

"You can tell me what clothes I require."

"Quite easily, and I have some guns aboard my yacht which you will find very useful."

"You will lend them to me? That is very kind of you, Uncle Tyrone."

There was a note of excitement in David's voice

which his uncle did not miss. Then in a different tone he said:

"Mother! What will she say?"

"I suggest you leave your mother to me," Tyrone Strome replied. "Do not say anything to her until I have talked to her, and incidentally I think as her guest I should go and find her now. We can do so together if you will allow me to get my coat."

"I will get it for you," David Merrill said. "It is in your room?"

"You will find it on the chair," his uncle answered.

David started towards the chalet, then he paused.

"By the way, Uncle Tyrone, that was pretty agile the way you dropped down from the balcony. I would think twice about doing that myself."

"And of course it is surprising in your decrepit old uncle," Tyrone Strome remarked with a note of amusement in his voice.

"I did not say that."

"But I am sure you thought it. Never mind. Get my coat and we will find your mother."

❋   ❋   ❋

"But, Tyrone, is it safe for David to go off to Africa with these men?"

"He has to grow up, Helene," her brother answered, "and from what I have overheard he is taking what I imagine is his first love-affair very seriously."

Helene Merrill sighed.

At forty-five she was still very beautiful and there were several men beseeching her to marry again, only to be refused, because, as her brother knew, she was so devoted to her only son.

"Nevada Van Arden is very lovely," she sighed. "One can understand David and quite a number of other young men losing their heads over her."

"She sounded, from what I heard of her conversation with David, one of the most unpleasant examples of heartless, frivolous modernity I have encountered for some time," Tyrone Strome replied.

His sister looked startled.

"I suppose you think that because you have not seen her."

"What had happened to her, by the way, when I joined your party?"

"She rushed off in a car with several neighbours. I did not approve, but she did not exactly ask my permission."

"In spite of the fact that she is staying in your house? Extraordinarily bad manners, if nothing else."

Lady Merrill smiled.

"You are being very old-fashioned, Tyrone. American girls like Nevada have an independence which is denied their poor English counterparts."

"You forget I know nothing about her."

Lady Merrill smiled again.

"Then let me tell you that Nevada Van Arden is one of the richest heiresses in America."

"I realised she was American, and with all that money she has naturally been excessively spoilt."

"I am afraid that is true," Lady Merrill said, "but her mother, who was at school with me, was one of the sweetest and gentlest people I have ever known. Elizabeth was the daughter of the Earl of Fenbridge and she married Clint Van Arden a year after her début. I believe she was very happy."

Tyrone Strome was listening with a somewhat cynical smile on his lips as his sister continued:

"We used to write to each other, although it is always difficult to keep up a friendship with a person on the other side of the Atlantic. Then when Nevada was eight or nine Elizabeth died, and Clint Van Arden was, I believe, brokenhearted."

"Who told you that?"

"Oh, a lot of my American friends," Lady Merrill answered. "He concerned himself only with making money, and I imagine had little time for his only child."

"You are trying to make me feel sorry for her," Tyrone Strome said accusingly, "but, quite frankly, Helene, pity is the last thing I would offer her."

"I think she would be insulted if you did," Lady Merrill replied. "She is very sure of herself, quite convinced that the world is there for her to walk on. But the thing is that she does not walk on ordinary soil but on hearts."

She saw the expression of contempt in her brother's eyes and went on:

"Wait until you see her. When you do so, you will understand why my poor David and other young men like him have not a chance."

Lady Merrill paused, then said with a throb in her voice:

"Oh, Tyrone, I have been so worried about him."

"I can understand that," her brother replied.

He had not told his sister of David's threat to take his life or the fact that he had found him actually with a revolver in his hand. But perhaps Lady Merrill knew more than he thought, because after a moment she said:

"I think you are right, Tyrone. If David goes away he will perhaps forget Nevada."

"I have no wish for him to forget her," Tyrone Strome said. "What I want him to realise is how shallow and worthless she is."

His voice sharpened as he said:

"I cannot imagine how a man with any sense in his head would want to marry a creature without any attribute that is essentially feminine."

His sister smiled.

"There have been many feminine women in your life, Tyrone, but you have never married."

"I have never found anyone as attractive as you to look at or to talk to, my dear."

She laughed.

"You flatter me!"

"No, I am speaking the truth. I find women alluring until I have to listen to their conversation. I find them extremely desirable until they try to interfere with my way of living."

"But, Tyrone, you cannot be a bachelor for the rest of your life."

"Why not?"

"Because it would be such a waste, and I would love to see you with children of your own."

Lady Merrill sighed.

"I regret so bitterly that I had only one child. I would have loved a dozen, but as you know, after David was born the Doctor said there could be no more."

Tyrone put out his hand and laid it on his sister's.

"It is too late for children, Helene, but I would like to see you happily married again. There are, I am sure, a number of applicants for the position."

His sister smiled.

"One or two, but I feel I should devote myself to David until he settles down. There is sometimes a wild streak in him that makes me afraid."

"It is part of growing up, Helene, and a husband would help you to understand David and to manage him."

"I certainly would not have thought of sending him to Africa."

"It will be the saving of him, even though I know it will hurt you to part with him."

"If I am honest, I think I should be glad for him to go if he can forget Nevada Van Arden. She has made him so desperately miserable and now she is doing the same to young Dundonald."

"Gerald's son?" Tyrone asked.

"Yes, you remember him? Such a nice boy."

Lady Merrill paused, then said:

"Of course there is no reason why she should not marry him: he will be a Marquis one day. I suppose all Americans like titles."

"So that is what she is after—in which case why not David?"

"I do not know, unless she thinks a Marquis is a better catch."

There was a note of bitterness in Lady Merrill's voice which made her brother tighten his lips. Then with an effort she said:

"Talking of titles, Tyrone, I am told that you refused the K.C.M.G.—why?"

"Who has been talking?"

"Someone who knows and admires you enormously."

"Then they should be intelligent enough to keep their mouths shut."

"Then it is true—you were offered the K.C.M.G.?"

"I might have been," Tyrone said evasively, "but I made it very clear that I am not interested in titles or decorations."

"It would have made me very proud of you."

"Do I really need a title for you to feel like that?"

"No, of course not. You know I think you are wonderful—I always have! There has never been anyone like you, Tyrone, but I would like the whole world to realise what an exceptional person you are."

Tyrone Strome laughed and rose to his feet.

"You are becoming spoilt by social standards," he said. "When I go to London and when I come to the Riviera I realise how very small is this glittering little world within the world."

"I suppose that is true," his sister admitted, "and whatever you do or do not do, Tyrone, I love you. You have always been the kindest and most wonderful brother any woman could have."

"Then trust me to do what is right for David."

"I am trusting you, and I am sure—really sure— you are right."

"I know I am."

Tyrone Strome rose from the chair on which he had been sitting to kiss his sister's cheek.

"Go to bed, dearest," he said. "We will talk everything over in the morning, but do not forget that David will have to leave on the two-o'clock train."

"Ronaldson will see to everything," Lady Merrill said. "I heard David telling him before we came upstairs to have everything ready."

"Ronaldson will not fail. He has never failed any of us," Tyrone smiled. "Good-night, my dear. Try to sleep. There are few problems that cannot be solved by the morning."

He gave her what she thought was an irresistible smile as he went from her bed-room.

Tyrone Strome walked downstairs preparatory to going to his own room.

It was very late, or rather early in the morning, and the servants, having cleared up after the dinner-dance, had gone to bed.

The Villa was very quiet but the lights in the hall had been left on and shone on the huge vases of arum lilies standing on the side-tables.

They always seemed to Tyrone Strome to be an emblem of purity and he knew that he looked for-ward to seeing them whenever he returned to the South of France.

His eyes were in fact on the lilies, which had been skillfully arranged to display their exquisite beauty at its best, when the front door opened and someone came in.

He turned his head to see who it was and saw that it was a girl.

She was wearing a white wrap over a white gown and at first glance she seemed to be as pure and per-fect as the lilies at which he had been looking.

Having shut the door behind her, she took off the white chiffon scarf which covered her head and he saw that her hair was the flaming vivid red so loved by the Viennese painters.

She had a small heart-shaped face with perfect features and huge eyes that seemed almost too large to be real.

He thought they were dark, then as she moved he realised in the light that they were green.

The girl was looking at him and Tyrone Strome was aware that they were both staring at each other in a manner that had something significant about it. Then she said:

"Who are you?"

It was only then as he heard her voice that he knew who she was.

"I am Tyrone Strome," he answered, "Lady Merrill's brother and—David's uncle."

He accentuated the last two words and there was a faint smile on Nevada's red lips as she replied:

"Of course! You were expected yesterday. David has told me quite a lot about you."

"I have heard a lot about you, too, Miss Van Arden."

"And everything, I am certain, to my *dis*advantage."

"Exactly!"

The word was spoken quietly, and yet somehow it sounded an insult.

She looked at him from under her eye-lashes, which were very long and dark and turned up at the ends.

"So the explorer, the adventurer, the gentleman whose exploits are veiled in mystery, is disposed to be critical!"

"Can you expect me to be anything else?"

"I expect nothing, Mr. Strome. It is simply amusing to know that you are prejudiced."

"Only as regards certain people."

"And me in particular."

Nevada made a little gesture with her hand which he had to admit was very graceful.

"You put yourself in a position, Miss Van Arden, which leaves you open to criticism."

"Which I find far preferable to being a nonentity and making no impact at all on the people I meet."

"I am sure that would be quite impossible."

The words were not a compliment, and as he saw the laughter in her eyes he had a feeling that she was deliberately trying to incite and provoke him.

Her next words confirmed the impression.

"You have lived in the wilds for so long, Mr. Strome, that I think you are out of touch with civilisation. Let me assure you that tomorrow it will be amusing to expose your ignorance and find flaws in such an acclaimed hero!"

Every word, spoken softly, was a rapier-thrust.

Then she moved towards the stairs and as she passed him he smelt the fragrance of tuberoses, which he thought scornfully was a very inappropriate perfume for a girl to use.

"Good-night, Mr. Strome," she said with her hand on the bannisters. "I shall look forward to meeting you again, but you must forgive me if I say that so far I find you disappointing."

Her green eyes were undoubtedly provocative and her lips curved over the words.

She moved slowly up the stairs with the grace of a Queen, conscious with every movement, Tyrone Strome was sure, that he was watching her.

When he heard the door of her bed-room close behind her he found himself laughing.

There was no doubt that Miss Van Arden, unpleasant, hard, and exemplifying everything he disliked in a modern girl, was in appearance, if nothing else, very different from what he had expected her to be.

"No wonder," he said to himself, "that poor English David is hypnotised by this exotic serpent—or rather, with her red hair, would not a more appropriate simile be a vixen?"

As he walked back to his chalet Tyrone Strome was thinking of the cruel, unpleasant manner in which she had spoken to his nephew and of the boy's misery and despair.

He was well aware that if he had not arrived when he had, if he had not overheard the conversation from the balcony, David might have been provoked into an action which would have broken his mother's heart.

It was sheer chance that he had been able to prevent such a tragedy, and as he reached his room Tyrone Strome said aloud:

"Damn the little vixen! She needs a sharp lesson and I hope to God that one day she gets it!"

Chapter Two

Tyrone Strome was having breakfast on the terrace outside his chalet.

He had risen early as he always did and was finding the cool of the morning, with the sunshine paler than it would be later in the day, an enchantment.

He had always loved the vivid colours of the Mediterranean and he thought as he had often done before that nothing could be more attractive than the view from his chalet, the tinkle of a fountain in the garden below and the exotic blossoms climbing over the balustrade in front of him.

He had gone to sleep thinking of his sister's problems with regard to her son but had slept deeply and dreamlessly, and this morning he felt vividly aware of his good health and high spirits.

Part of it, he knew, was relief from no longer being oppressed by the seriousness of his mission or the danger he was in.

The past years in fact had made him feel older than he actually was and now he felt like a schoolboy starting his holidays, sure that he was going to enjoy every minute of them.

He thought as he helped himself from a plate of fish that had been caught the previous day that once David had set out for Africa he would enjoy being alone with his sister and talking to her as they had not been able to do for twelve months.

He had not been flattering her when he said that he found her more intelligent and indeed more attractive than any other woman he knew.

He loved Helene because she was sympathetic and both in her appearance and in her outlook a very feminine woman.

Tyrone Strome had lived a tough and what many people thought a hard life, and it had taught him to be ruthless and at times cruel.

In contrast, when he was with a woman, he wanted everything about her to be soft and yielding.

This was what he had demanded of any woman with whom he had a love-affair, and he knew when he thought about her that Nevada Van Arden typified everything he disliked in the modern girl.

Almost as if the thought of her conjured her up, he heard footsteps behind him and turned his head to see David and Nevada together advancing towards him over the carefully watered green lawns.

Silhouetted against the dark cypress trees, Nevada looked, as she had last night, ethereal and very lovely.

She was not wearing a hat and the sun glinting on her hair turned it into tongues of fire.

Her eyes were very green against the translucency of her white skin.

Slowly, annoyed that he should be interrupted at breakfast-time, Tyrone Strome rose to his feet.

"Good-morning, Uncle Tyrone," David said, and there was an unmistakable touch of nervousness in his voice.

"Good-morning, David, good-morning, Miss Van Arden," Tyrone Strome said. "Will you forgive me if I go on with my breakfast? You are both surprisingly early."

"We came to see you because Ronaldson told me you are going to Nice," David said.

"That is what I intend to do," Tyrone Strome answered. "As I told you last night, I have some guns aboard my yacht and also other equipment which you will find useful in Africa."

"I did not wish you to take an unnecessary journey," David said.

The words were spoken almost hesitantly. Then with a triumphant note in her voice Nevada interposed:

"What David is trying to tell you, Mr. Strome, is that he is not going."

Her green eyes were on his as she spoke, and Tyrone Strome knew that the expression in them was deliberately provocative.

He raised his eye-brows but said nothing as David explained rather uncomfortably:

"I wrote a note to Nevada last night and told her I was going to Africa, but this morning she has persuaded me to stay here and look after her. It was what I had promised to do."

"Then naturally you must keep your promise," Tyrone Strome replied.

If David expected him to protest—if they thought he would show anger or irritation at his nephew's change of mind—he was determined that they would be disappointed.

"There, David, I told you you were working yourself into a frenzy for nothing!" Nevada remarked.

As she spoke she reached out and took a piece of toast from the silver rack on the breakfast-table, spread it with butter, and added a spoonful of honey.

She bit into it with her pearly white teeth.

"Delicious!" she said. "I cannot think why I did not ask for honey. I forgot how good it is in this part of the world."

David was looking at his uncle.

"I do not want you to think I am ungrateful, Uncle Tyrone, for what you suggested last night. Ronaldson told me that you have already sent a telegram to your friends. I am sorry about that, but of course I wish to stay if Nevada wants me."

"Of course I want you," Nevada said. "I naturally need a handsome and distinguished escort to dance with and to take me to all the fascinating places there are to see around here."

"Yesterday you said they bored you," David remarked.

"That was yesterday," Nevada replied with a wave of her hand. "Today I have changed my mind. We must make plans, David, to explore all the interesting places in the neighbourhood."

"Will you be content to do so in one of Mama's carriages?" David asked. "Or are you going to insist on going in that noisy, smelly car of Charlie's?"

"That is certainly a thought," Nevada answered. "Incidentally, it is not smelly and it is very fast."

"Much too fast!" David said sullenly. "It is dangerous, as you well know, to travel at any speed on these roads."

"I like living dangerously," Nevada answered. "Mr. Strome will agree with that . . . will you not?"

She looked directly at Tyrone Strome as she spoke, opening her green eyes with a deliberately contrived expression of innocence in them and making her question sound ingenuous and flattering.

Tyrone Strome looked at her with a glint of amusement in his eyes.

"I wonder, Miss Van Arden, if you have any idea of what danger means?"

"Not unless you are referring to being alone on a moonlit deck with a very attractive man," she replied.

"When did that happen to you?" David asked jealously. "You never told me."

"My dear David, you cannot expect me to confess all the interludes that occur in my life," Nevada replied. "Besides, you know I dislike men who are jealous."

"How can you expect me to be anything else?"

"I find jealousy, like love, an emotion I can do without," Nevada replied lightly. "They are both extremely inhibiting to enjoyment, and, make no mistake, I am determined to enjoy myself."

David was looking at her with an expression of hopeless yearning.

It was not surprising, Tyrone Strome told himself, that the boy was infatuated, for Nevada was undoubtedly one of the loveliest creatures he had ever seen in his life.

It was a pity that she was also, he thought, one of the most unpleasant specimens of her kind that it had ever been his misfortune to encounter.

He was well aware that she was attempting to show him her power over David and to flout his authority in a manner which told him all too clearly she would stop at nothing to get her own way.

"I suppose, Mr. Strome," she said as she finished the toast and honey, "it would be useless to include you in our plans for today?"

"Is that an invitation?" he asked.

He spoke in a manner which surprised her.

She glanced at him quickly and his long experience with women told him that for the first time she regarded him as a possible conquest.

"Why not?" she asked. "You know that I would love hearing about your exploits . . . if you are prepared to talk to me about them."

She almost overdid the eagerness of a young girl encountering a celebrity, Tyrone Strome thought cynically, but he answered:

"I should be afraid, after all you have said about wishing to be amused, that you might find them dull."

"I am sure nothing you could do would ever be dull, Mr. Strome."

"Adventures, however unpredictable, can have their dull moments, especially if one is alone," he answered.

"Then we must certainly try to make up to you for the times that you have felt lonely," Nevada said softly.

"I am flattered," Tyrone Strome smiled, "but I

must not impose myself upon you and David. I am sure you have so many things to do together and if I accompanied you I should be very much *de trop.*"

"No, no, of course you would not!" Nevada said quickly. "We would like to have you, would we not, David?"

"If you say so," David replied without much enthusiasm.

Tyrone Strome could have laughed aloud at the way this inexperienced young woman thought she was on the point of captivating him.

He had flirted with some of the most alluring, sophisticated, and famous beauties in the world, and he was not for one second deceived by the wide-eyed ingenuousness that Nevada had now assumed for his benefit.

He was also well aware that his nephew was looking at him suspiciously, already jealous of Nevada's interest in him.

"I think perhaps I had better first find out what your mother wants to do, David," Tyrone Strome said. "She did speak of visiting my yacht."

"Oh, I would love to see it, too!" Nevada cried. "Would you show it to me? I have a passion for yachts."

"But of course," he answered. "It would be a very great pleasure to show you over the *Moulay.*"

"Is that what you call her?"

"Yes; it means, as you may not know, 'Sovereign,' in Arabic. I consider my yacht a King among other vessels."

"Then I must certainly see her immediately!" Nevada said imperiously. "Please persuade Lady Merrill to take us all to the *Moulay.*"

"Have you forgotten you asked me to send a note to Charles telling him I would come over to his Villa to play tennis before luncheon this morning?" David said sulkily. "I expect by now the groom will have left with it."

"So I did," Nevada answered. "Well, we can send another to say that after all you are too busy."

Tyrone Strome had the idea that she had been making arrangements to take David's mind off the fact that he was altering his plans to go to Africa.

"Perhaps the groom has not yet left," she said quickly. "Go and see, David, and find out if you can stop him."

"All right," David agreed, "but Charles will be disappointed."

"I will console him later," Nevada said lightly.

David, who had been sitting on the arm of a chair near the breakfast-table, rose and walked back towards the Villa.

Nevada waited until he was out of sight, then she said:

"Perhaps I made a mistake in stopping David from following your advice. It might have been more amusing without him."

There was an innuendo in her voice which made Tyrone Strome long to spank her, instead of which he said suavely:

"I thought it would interest him to do some big-game shooting."

"And of course he would forget me! It is the standard solution for a young man in love with some-one unsuitable."

"Did I say that you were unsuitable?" Tyrone Strome asked.

"You made that obvious last night."

"Perhaps my judgement was too hasty and based on hearsay."

"And now you have changed your mind?"

"Are we still talking about David?"

Tyrone Strome was playing the game of duelling with words, when every sentence had an ulterior meaning and each one was as sharp as the point of a rapier.

"I think, Mr. Strome, I am a little frightened of you," Nevada said.

Her lips curved over the words and she deliberately dropped her eyes in a manner which to a less experienced man would have seemed enticingly young and shy.

"I am sure you are nothing of the sort," Tyrone Strome replied. "I feel, Miss Van Arden, we have a lot to learn about each other."

"I would like you to call me Nevada. 'Miss Van Arden' sounds so formal."

"You are very gracious."

Only those who knew Tyrone Strome very well would have realised that he was not only being sarcastic but also there was an impish light in his eyes which showed that he was enjoying himself.

He had not forgotten for one moment that last night he had saved David from an action that might at this moment have shrouded the whole Villa and everyone in it in the deepest misery.

He was determined to fight this vixen of a girl with her own weapons, and he knew, despite the fact that she had come out into the garden to crow over him, hating him because he had shown himself last night to be critical, that she was now thinking that she would have her revenge by making him her slave.

It was quite understandable that she was used to men falling head-over-heels in love with her on sight and becoming like David so infatuated that they lost all sense of proportion.

There was no doubt about her beauty, but Tyrone Strome thought it was a beauty that was as evil and pernicious as that of Medusa, who had at least warned men of her wickedness by wearing her hair filled with snakes.

Nevada's hair had an enticement that was all its own, and he knew that most men would find it impossible not to lose their heads when she looked at them from under her dark lashes and her green eyes seemed to hold all the mysteries of the East.

"I wish we had talked for a little longer last night," Nevada said in a sweet voice, "but of course there are other nights, and the moonlight makes this one of the most romantic places I have ever visited."

"That is what I think myself," Tyrone Strome agreed.

"Then perhaps we could look at it together," she suggested softly.

"Why not?" he enquired. "But we must not waste the hours of sunlight."

"No, of course not," she answered, "and I would like to see your yacht."

She looked at him for a moment, before she said:

"I will make David play tennis. He will only be a bore, mooning about after us when there is so much I want you to tell me, so much I would like you to explain."

"What a good idea!" Tyrone Strome exclaimed. "You go and arrange things with David and I will go and talk to my sister."

He rose from the breakfast-table as he spoke and Nevada rose too.

Every movement that she made had a grace that was all its own, and he thought in her white gown and with her gleaming red hair it was hard to believe that she was as dangerous as he had learnt her to be from the first moment of their acquaintance.

He smiled in a way that women had found beguiling ever since he had been in the cradle.

"I shall look forward to being your host on the *Moulay*."

"It will be very exciting!" Nevada replied with that glance from under her eye-lashes which Tyrone Strome was quite certain she had practised in front of a mirror.

They walked slowly side by side towards the Villa.

They had almost reached the long white steps leading up to it when David came running down them.

"It is no use, Nevada," he said, "the note has gone, but I can send the groom back with another as soon as he returns."

"I think that would be needlessly unkind . . ." Nevada began.

Tyrone Strome did not wait to hear any more.

He left the two of them talking together and went up to his sister's room.

He knew she did not rise early, and in fact he found her sitting up in bed wearing a blue chiffon dressing-jacket and looking young and very attractive against a pile of lace-edged pillows.

"Good-morning, Tyrone dearest," she said. "I was hoping you would come to see me."

He bent to kiss her cheek, then sat down on the edge of the bed to take her hand in his.

"You slept well?" she asked. "You are looking extremely handsome this morning. I am looking forward to introducing you to my friends so that they will see what a charming brother I have."

"Unfortunately, I have bad news for you."

He felt her stiffen, then he said:

"That girl, Nevada, has persuaded David not to go to Africa."

"Oh, no!" Lady Merrill exclaimed. "I was thinking it over last night, Tyrone, and was certain it was the right thing for him to do. He has been so miserable, so unhappy ever since she came here."

"I can understand that."

"One moment she encourages him, the next minute she snubs him and crushes him in a manner that is so unnecessarily cruel that I can hardly bear to watch it happening."

"Why do you think she behaves like that?"

"I suppose it is to show off her power. She is the same with every man she meets. She has to have them grovelling at her feet. Lord Dundonald is feeling nearly as desperate about Charles as I am about David."

"How long did you invite her to stay?"

"For another three weeks!" Lady Merrill said. "Heaven knows what damage she will have done by then!"

It was a cry that her brother could well understand, remembering what had nearly happened last night.

"Surely she has not travelled from America alone?" he asked.

"No, of course not!" Lady Merrill answered. "Her father sent an elderly woman with her, who I believe is very nice, although I am quite certain she was completely ineffective as a Chaperon where Nevada was concerned."

"What happened to her?" Tyrone Strome enquired.

"She was ill when they reached London. When I invited Nevada to stay, having no idea what she was like, I naturally asked them both to be my guests."

"But the Chaperon did not come?"

"No, Nevada wrote and explained that she would come alone and arranged for a Courier to escort her on the journey."

Lady Merrill made a little gesture with her hands.

"As I have already told you, she is very efficient when it comes to looking after herself, and I believe she has travelled quite a lot in the past."

"So she arrived alone," Tyrone Strome said.

"Yes, she left her lady's-maid to look after Mrs. Langholme, or whatever her name is, and asked me to find her a French replacement for the time she was with us."

"So she will be here with you for a further three weeks," Tyrone Strome said reflectively.

His sister looked uncomfortable.

"If I am honest I must tell you that I said in the letter three weeks or as long as she wished. I had no idea then that Elizabeth's daughter would be like this, or indeed so beautiful."

Lady Merrill sighed.

"One cannot deny her beauty, but it is the way she uses it that is so disturbing. Oh, Tyrone, do try to persuade David to go away."

"Nevada has informed him that she wants him here to escort and amuse her."

Lady Merrill put her hands up to her eyes.

"I cannot imagine what David will be like at the

end of her visit. He is making himself ill over the girl.
Ronaldson tells me that he walks about half the night
smoking, which he never did before, and you will
notice at meals that he hardly eats anything."

Tyrone Strome did not speak and Lady Merrill
reached out towards him.

"Talk to him, Tyrone, perhaps he will listen to
you. It is times like this when I feel so helpless and
wish with all my heart that George was alive."

"I wonder if David would have listened to his
father," Tyrone Strome said, "or to anyone else."

"Then what are we to do?"

There was a fear in Lady Merrill's eyes which
made her brother feel very protective towards her.

Because his sister was considerably older, he had
always felt that he could rely on her; yet now she was
appealing to him in a manner that he knew he could
not refuse.

He rose from the bed to walk to the window and
although he was looking at the view he did not see it.

He was thinking, calculating, working out a plan
with a concentration which those who had served with
him in one capacity or another knew made him one
of the most formidable adversaries the enemies of
Great Britain had ever encountered.

To Tyrone it was an exercise in will-power, and,
although he never spoke of it, it was a kind of reaching out within himself for help when it was really
necessary.

He could not describe exactly what happened
when there seemed to be no solution to a problem or
he was in a situation in which it seemed he must be
defeated.

Then something within himself cried out for help,
and help came in a manner that perhaps other people
would describe as miraculous.

Almost as if he saw the details falling into place
like a military operation, he knew now exactly what
he must do, what action he must take.

The power had been given to him.

He turned round to find his sister looking at him

beseechingly. He smiled at her and she knew that once again, as he had done so often before in his life, he had found a solution.

"I want you to order a carriage for eleven-thirty A.M.," he said, "to take you and Nevada to Cannes."

Lady Merrill looked at him in surprise, but she did not speak as he went on explaining to her exactly what he wanted her to do.

* * *

Driving into Cannes in an open Victoria drawn by a perfectly matched pair of horses, Lady Merrill chatted to the girl beside her about the dance they were to attend that evening.

"We are dining at the Villa," she said, "and afterwards we go on to Lady Byng's. I have promised to bring a party of twenty and if all our friends do the same it should be quite an amusing evening."

"I am sure it will be," Nevada replied. "Does your brother, Mr. Strome, enjoy dancing?"

"I think Tyrone dances superbly, as he does everything else that is athletic," Lady Merrill answered. "He is an expert skier, an outstanding polo-player, and was as a boy a very fine cricketer."

"So many talents in one person!" Nevada remarked.

Lady Merrill was not certain if it was a compliment or a criticism.

"I have always been very proud of Tyrone," she said, "and of course, because he is so attractive and so rich, he has a great number of female admirers, despite the fact that he is very much a man's man."

"Why has he never married?"

"That is a question I have often asked him myself," Lady Merrill replied, "but he is very fastidious and although I know a great number of beautiful women who would gladly be his wife, he never makes any effort to wed."

"Perhaps he is waiting to fall in love."

There was no doubt that the remark was mocking.

"Is not that what we all want?" Lady Merrill enquired.

"It is something that will never happen to me," Nevada said. "I find love a nauseating weakness which disgusts me."

"My dear child, you cannot really mean that!"

"It is true," Nevada said defiantly, "and I expect that no-one will believe it until I become an old maid, doubtless in the last years of my life devoting myself to good works."

"You can only be joking."

"No, I am not," Nevada answered. "I cannot imagine myself in the state that men get into when they tell me they are in love with me, trembling with swimming eyes and trying to paw me with hot hands. It makes me sick!"

"Your mother never talked like that! She wanted to fall in love and be married, and have lots of children. I am sure for her it was a tragedy that like me she could have only one."

"Perhaps she was bored with the whole idea after I was born."

"I am sure that is not true," Lady Merrill contradicted. "I have never had the chance of discussing such things with your father, but I am quite certain if your mother could have given you a brother or a sister she would have been thrilled to do so."

"I suppose my father would have liked a son," Nevada answered in a hard voice, "but he was not particularly interested in his daughter."

"I am sure that is not true," Lady Merrill said gently, "and, Nevada, let me give you a little word of advice: if you want love you have to give love."

"But I do not want it!" Nevada said sharply. "It is the last thing I want! I am very content as I am, but nobody seems to realise it. I enjoy myself and if men like to make fools of themselves over me, why should I worry about them? They are quite capable of taking care of themselves."

"But are they?" Lady Merrill asked. "That is really

the question that a mother asks. Can a young man who is desperately, wildly in love with someone like you understand that you have no interest in him except as a possible dancing partner?"

"I have already told you, Lady Merrill, men must learn to look after themselves. They are big and strong enough."

Nevada spoke scornfully and Lady Merrill replied:

"I often think that the trouble is that men never really grow up. They are all little boys at heart, especially to their mothers. They want to be looked after, loved, given encouragement and inspiration."

Nevada laughed.

"I can inspire anyone I wish," she said boastfully, "but I have no intention of looking after a man or allowing one to look after me. They are fools, every one of them. They are only amusing before they fall in love—not after."

Lady Merrill lapsed into silence.

The horses drove along the esplanade bordered with pine trees towards the harbour at the end of the town.

It was only a small harbour but it was filled with yachts of all sizes, and Nevada looked eagerly for the *Moulay,* the yacht belonging to Tyrone Strome.

She had a feeling that it would be different from the others and she was not mistaken.

Instead of being all white as were those belonging to rich French, English, and Italian owners, the *Moulay* had a prow of black picked out in gold.

She also had a deep black line above the watermark and appeared longer, thinner, and more graceful than any of the other yachts moored near her.

As the horses drew to a standstill beside the gang-plank Lady Merrill said:

"It is not yet twelve o'clock. What I would like to do, Nevada, is to drop in at the Carlton Hotel and call on my friend the Duchess of Westbourne, who has been ill. I will not be long. Will you tell my brother that I will join you both before luncheon?"

"I will give him your message, Lady Merrill," Nevada answered.

The footman had climbed down from the box of the carriage to open the door and she stepped out, realising as she put her foot on the gang-plank that Tyrone was waiting on deck.

The carriage drove away as she stepped aboard holding out her hand and saying as he took it:

"Your sister asked me to tell you she is calling on the Duchess of Westbourne and will return before luncheon."

"How very tactful of her!" Tyrone Strome replied in his deep voice. "That means I shall have the pleasure of showing you everything alone."

"That will be delightful," Nevada smiled.

She was well aware that she was looking exceedingly attractive in a gown of white muslin trimmed with turquoise-blue ribbons slotted through broderie anglaise.

Her wide-brimmed hat was decorated with the same ribbons and bunches of forget-me-nots. She looked the epitome of a young girl until one looked into the smouldering depth of her green eyes, or noticed the enticement of her curved lips.

She went ahead of Tyrone Strome into the Saloon, which was decorated in a different manner from what she had expected aboard a luxury yacht.

Everything was very severe, masculine, and business-like.

There was no superfluous decoration, no soft cushions or pictures on the walls as there had been in every other yacht she had visited.

"I thought first we would both enjoy a cup of coffee," Tyrone Strome said as he followed her. "Do you like the Turkish variety? I have been so long in the East that I prefer it to the French."

"So do I," Nevada replied.

A steward appeared and Tyrone Strome spoke to him in a strange language which she did not recognise. Then looking at the man she thought he was Chinese.

When they were alone she asked:

"Why do you not employ English stewards?"

"All my crew are either Chinese or Malayan," Tyrone Strome replied. "They are excellent seamen and can adapt themselves to almost any conditions."

He smiled as he continued:

"We are not usually moored anywhere so luxurious as a harbour in the South of France!"

"Where has your yacht come from now?"

"It has been to many different parts of the world."

"Am I to assume from that answer that you do not intend to tell me anything more specific?" Nevada asked.

"Why should you be interested?" he enquired.

She laughed.

"You are treating me as if I were a spy from the other side, wherever that might be. Do you think I might perhaps be employed by the Russians?"

"I think you look too obviously dangerous for anyone who met you not to be forewarned and forearmed," Tyrone Strome replied.

"Are you paying me a compliment?"

"If you like to make it one."

They were duelling again and he knew she was enjoying it.

"I think you are making yourself unnecessarily enigmatic, Mr. Strome," she said. "I am rather suspicious of this cloak-and-dagger reputation you have acquired."

"Suspicious?" he questioned.

"It obviously makes you seem very intriguing. Is that why you deliberately cultivate a Sphinx-like attitude?"

"I do not often have time to think about myself," Tyrone Strome replied, "but now you make me feel as if the quality you describe is certainly an asset."

"That will not prevent me from trying to pin you down and make you tell me a great deal more about yourself."

"I should have to be very conceited to think that you were interested in me, when there are so many contenders for your attention."

"Shall I say there is always room for newcomers?" Nevada asked.

He did not have to reply, for at that moment the steward came back into the Saloon carrying a tray on which there were two handleless china cups set in holders of wrought gold decorated with turquoises.

"How pretty!" Nevada exclaimed.

"I was given them when I was in the East," Tyrone Strome explained.

The steward poured the thick sweet coffee into the cups and Nevada instantly raised hers to inspect the turquoises and the intricate work in which they were set.

"They are really beautiful!" she cried.

"If I were in the East and made the polite reply I would have to answer: 'They are yours!'" Tyrone Strome said. "But as it is I am selfish enough to wish to keep them for myself."

"How ungenerous of you," she pouted.

"If you had them, what would you do with them?" he enquired.

"Drink coffee out of them, of course," Nevada said. "This is delicious!"

"I have taught my Chef how to make it in the proper Turkish fashion: black as the devil, hot as hell, and sweet as love!"

"Do you really believe that love is sweet?" Nevada asked.

"It depends with whom one is in love," Tyrone Strome replied.

"You are as bad as your sister! She has been talking to me about love and I told her it is an emotion which I shall never feel and which I despise and dislike."

"How very unusual to find such a positive opinion in someone as young as yourself!"

"In one moment you are going to say I am too young to know my own mind," Nevada flashed.

"I hope I should not say anything so banal or so obviously untrue."

"Then you accept that I do know my own mind?"

"I am quite sure of it," Tyrone Strome replied. "You are a very positive person. It is only the indecisive and frustrated in this world who are afraid of their own thoughts."

"You are being so pleasant to me, Mr. Strome, that I am wondering if you have an ulterior motive," Nevada remarked.

"I cannot understand why you should think that," he replied.

As he spoke he refilled her cup with coffee.

She noticed he had not touched his and thought that perhaps despite what he had said he did not care for anything so sweet.

Not that it interested her. She was intent on making him talk and finding out what he thought about her.

"How many times have you been in love?" she asked provocatively.

"If I reply—Never!" Tyrone Strome said, "you would not believe me; while I have a feeling that if I answer—Many times! you will be even more inquisitive than you are already."

"You are very pleased with yourself!"

"Why not?" he asked. "I think we both have an appreciation of our own characters, our own capabilities, and more than anything else our own ambitions."

She looked at him in surprise.

"Do you think that I am ambitious?"

"Everyone is in one way or another."

Her brow wrinkled a little as she said:

"I feel you are not talking about the usual ambitions people have: a desire for money, a title, or success."

"That is perceptive of you, Nevada," Tyrone Strome said. "You must have a brain somewhere—although I had not suspected it until now."

She looked at him in surprise.

"That is almost insulting."

"I thought you would accept it as a compliment."

"Not in the way you said it."

"Then I must apologise. I thought you were the type of woman who preferred to be praised for your brain rather than your beauty."

"I am . . ."

She drew in her breath and said in a different tone of voice:

"Surely it is very hot in here?"

"It is going to be a hot day," Tyrone Strome replied. "I will open another port-hole."

He rose as he spoke.

As he did so he noticed that Nevada put her hand up to her forehead and closed her eyes.

With an effort she opened them again to say:

"I have a head-ache. Will you fetch me a glass of water?"

"Yes, of course," Tyrone Strome answered.

He moved towards the door but he was watching her as he did so.

Again her hand went up to her forehead and now almost as if she did not realise what she was doing and felt in need of air she pulled off her wide-brimmed hat and let it fall down on the ground beside her.

"Mr. Str . . . ome!"

She found it difficult to say his name and her voice seemed as if it came from a long distance.

Then as she looked at him across the cabin her eyes widened suddenly and he knew that a thought had come to her mind, a thought that made her want to cry out, to accuse him.

But even as her lips tried to form the words she fell forward, collapsing sideways on the sofa.

He waited for a moment. Then he picked her up in his arms and carrying her carefully took her out of the Saloon and along the narrow passageway.

The door of a cabin had been left ajar and he pushed it open with his foot.

Like the Saloon it was well furnished, but austerely, and he set Nevada down on the bunk.

Her arm trailed over the edge of it and he put it tidily beside her body. Then he pulled the curtains over the port-hole to keep out the sunlight and went out of the cabin, locking the door behind him.

He put the key in his pocket and going up on deck told one of his crew to call a hackney-carriage for him.

When it came he ordered it to drive him to the Carlton Hotel.

Chapter Three

Nevada opened her eyes, then shut them again as if she could not believe what she saw.

Her head felt heavy and thick, and her mouth was very dry.

She tried to swallow and found it difficult.

She felt as if her brain was coming back from a very long distance where it had been dark.

Now she was aware of herself and once again she opened her eyes.

The first thing she saw was her own luggage piled high in what seemed to be a confined space, then she was aware of the noise of engines and thought she must be on a train.

But why?

And why, if she was on a train, were her trunks not in the Guard's Van?

She stared for some time, finding it difficult to focus her eyes, but conscious that her head was aching almost intolerably.

She sat up. As she did so, she saw a port-hole and realised she was not on a train but in a ship.

It was then that the memory of Tyrone Strome came back to her.

She could see his face quite clearly, the expression in his eyes, the mocking twist to his lips.

She had been going to expostulate with him; go-

ing to accuse him of something. Then suddenly she
remembered.

The coffee!

She had been drugged, she was sure of it.

Nevada put her feet to the floor and with an effort rose to walk towards the port-hole.

She was unsteady and felt giddy, but somehow
she managed to reach it and looked out to see nothing
but sea—sea stretching away towards a blue horizon
where it met the sky.

What had happened? Where was she?

For a moment she thought she must be dreaming, then she turned round to see the great pile of her
luggage very solid and real against the fitted furni-
ture of the cabin.

There was a dressing-table with a number of
drawers, a wardrobe and other drawers on one wall
of the cabin, cunningly designed so that the top of
them constituted a table.

The bunk in which she had been lying was larger
than was usual, but it did not compare with the bed
she had occupied in the liner in which she had
crossed the Atlantic.

Everything was plain and workman-like and she
remembered now that the Saloon had been the same.

The engines appeared to be throbbing under her
feet and the noise of them now seemed to ask the
same question over and over again.

"Why? Why? Why?"

Why had Tyrone Strome drugged her and where
was he taking her?

She knew that she must find the answers because
the questions were being asked not by the engines
but by her brain.

She walked to the door of the cabin expecting to
find it locked.

She turned the handle and it opened. Then when
she would have stepped out into the passage she hesi-
tated.

As she had moved across the cabin she had had a

quick sight of her reflection in the mirror and now she went back to look at herself again.

When she did so she saw that her gown was creased and her hair untidy.

Perhaps she had been restless while unconscious.

She was also aware that she felt hot and frowsty and wondered how long she had lain in a drugged sleep.

Of one thing she was very aware, and that was that she was thirsty.

She looked round and saw that there was another door to the cabin and opening it she found that it led into a small bath-room.

This, she knew, was a luxury that was unusual aboard a private yacht. Usually one private bath-room was attached to the Master Suite, but the guests had to make do with a communal one.

In the bath-room there were two taps on the basin, one labelled "salt," the other "drinking water." Finding a glass, Nevada filled it and drank thirstily.

It took away the dryness in her mouth and now she saw that there was a "tub," as the Americans called it, in which she was certain she would have to wash in sea-water, but there was also a shower.

She looked at it for a moment, then making up her mind she went into the cabin, locked the outer door, and undressed.

After she had showered, her head-ache was much better.

She pulled open one of her trunks at random and found a fresh gown well packed between layers of tissue paper.

This she knew was the work of the French maids. But who had conveyed her luggage to Cannes and what explanation had been given at the Villa for her precipitate departure?

These were questions Nevada was determined to find answers to, and when finally she was dressed and had tidied her hair, using the gold-backed brushes which were fitted into her crocodile dressing-case, her reflection looked back at her from the mirror and there was the light of battle in her green eyes.

Nevertheless, as she unlocked the door of her cabin and went in search of Tyrone Strome she was, although she would never have admitted it, a little nervous.

It was hard to understand why he had behaved as he had, but Nevada was determined that he would have to give her a very plausible explanation combined with an apology.

She went along the passage-way to the Saloon.

She half-expected that Tyrone Strome would be on deck, but he was in the Saloon seated at a flat-topped desk and he was writing.

He looked up as she entered but there was no surprise on his face, only an expression of gravity that she had not seen before.

She advanced towards him and although she knew that she was looking attractive there was no glint of admiration in his eyes which she expected from any man.

"So you are awake!"

"Yes, I am awake," Nevada replied, "and I wish to know why I am here and why you drugged me."

"It saved a lot of argument," he answered quietly.

"About what?"

"You might not have wished to leave Cannes as I intended that you should."

"Where are you taking me? This is a most extraordinary way to behave!"

"Extraordinary situations demand extraordinary actions," Tyrone Strome answered.

They were both standing, but now the ship gave a lurch and Nevada sat down in a high-back chair which was beside the desk.

She was, Tyrone Strome knew, keeping a tight control on herself, but he was aware of the anger in her eyes.

"I think, Mr. Strome," she said coldly, "you had better tell me what you think you are doing before

I order you to turn your yacht around and take me back to Cannes."

Tyrone Strome seated himself behind his desk, leaning back in an arm-chair, very much at his ease.

"I am taking you to Africa!" he said. "I think it could prove to be an essential part of your education."

"To . . . Africa?" Nevada exclaimed in astonishment.

She somehow vaguely imagined that they were crossing the Mediterranean perhaps to Malta or the Balearic Islands.

"This is ridiculous!" she said crossly. "You know as well as I do that you cannot take me away without explaining why I am leaving your sister, with whom I am staying."

"If you will allow me to be frank," Tyrone Strome answered, "my sister was exceedingly glad to get rid of you."

"You mean Lady Merrill . . . connived this . . . this kidnapping?"

"If you like to put it that way—yes."

"I have never heard anything so disgraceful in my whole life! As she had been a friend of my mother's, I thought I could trust her to treat me decently. I cannot imagine what my father will say when he hears of your behaviour!"

"He is unlikely to hear anything for a month or two," Tyrone Strome replied, "and as to my sister's involvement, you should realise by this time that just as a tigress will fight for her cubs so any mother will fight for her son."

"So your concern for David is at the bottom of all this nonsense!"

"Exactly!" Tyrone Strome agreed. "My very grave concern for David."

"And do you think he will let me disappear in this extraordinary manner, without wondering what has happened to me?"

"David is at this moment also on his way to Africa, but your paths will not meet."

"You forced him to go after he had promised to stay with me?"

"He was quite willing to do so after he had read your letter."

"What letter?"

"The letter you wrote him; a very charming one telling him that after he had left the Villa to play tennis you received an urgent message from your father asking you to return to America immediately."

Nevada stared at Tyrone Strome wide-eyed.

"You went on to say," he continued, "that while you will always be grateful for his friendship you have decided that your heart lies in the land where you were born, where you have always intended to live."

He paused before with his eyes on Nevada's face he said:

"It was a kind letter, the sort that a young man would treasure, and which would not leave him unhappy or distressed to the point where he might wish to take his life."

"You wrote that and signed it with my name?"

Nevada seemed almost to spit the words.

"Your hand-writing is quite easy to copy. There is nothing very difficult or indeed original about it."

"So you commit forgery amongst other crimes!"

"An accomplishment I have found very useful at various times in my life."

"How dare you behave in such a manner to me!"

"You made it impossible for me to do otherwise."

"Do you really believe those ridiculous threats David made of taking his own life?"

"I not only believe them, I actually saved him just in time from putting them into execution," Tyrone Strome answered, and his voice was hard.

"I do not believe you. Men who threaten suicide are only play-acting."

"Your experience of men is not as great as mine."

This was irrefutably true, and Nevada, her anger rising, said:

"It still does not excuse your behaviour in bringing me here, drugging me with your filthy coffee, and writing letters in my name. I insist that you turn this yacht around and take me back to France."

She saw the refusal in his face before he spoke, and conceded:

"If you are too frightened for your precious nephew to take me back to Cannes you can drop me at Marseilles. I have had enough of you and your family. I will go back to England."

"That might be possible," Tyrone Strome said, "except for one thing."

"What is that?"

"I have decided you need a lesson which will teach you not to hurt any other young men as you tried to hurt my nephew. David has escaped—others might not be so lucky."

"You are ridiculous! Absurd! Men are perfectly capable of looking after themselves. If not, they should not call themselves men."

"That is true where the ordinary woman is concerned. But you are not ordinary, Nevada. You are cruel, hard-hearted, and, I am almost inclined to think —evil!"

Nevada jumped to her feet.

"How dare you say such things to me! You are insulting, and your behaviour, as you well know, is criminal. You will go to prison, Mr. Strome, for behaving like this."

"That of course is a risk I have fully calculated," he answered, "but where at the moment can you find a policeman either French, English, or American? I do not as a rule carry one as part of the crew."

She stood looking at him. He knew she was considering what her next move would be but was finding it difficult to come to a decision.

After a moment she walked across the Saloon to stand at the port-hole looking out to sea.

"Where are we? How long have I been unconscious?"

"We are at the moment about twenty miles past Gibraltar," Tyrone Strome replied, "and moving along the Atlantic coast of Morocco. You were unconscious for approximately forty-eight hours."

"As long as that?"

"The drug I gave you is very effective. As you realise, it acts almost instantaneously."

There was something in the calm, quiet answers and the fact that Tyrone Strome's voice was almost expressionless that was rather awe-inspiring.

Petulantly Nevada flung herself onto the sofa.

"As I have had nothing to eat for forty-eight hours I am naturally very hungry."

"I can understand that," Tyrone Strome said, "but I have something to explain to you."

"What is that?"

"I brought you on this voyage not only to save my nephew and incidentally young Dundonald also, but to find out if it would be possible to turn a vixen into a woman."

"I do not . . . understand what you are trying to say to me."

"I think you do. You have gone through life up until now, Nevada, giving orders to people who have had to obey you because you paid them. What I intend to find out is if you have anything to give a man or woman except your money."

Vaguely at the back of her mind Nevada felt she had heard these words before. Then she remembered what she had said to David in the garden on the night of Tyrone Strome's arrival.

"You were listening!" she said accusingly. "I might have guessed what happened. You were listening in your room and David and I were below you in the garden."

"Yes, I was listening," Tyrone Strome admitted, "and I have never in my life heard a woman of any age so unpleasant, so unfeeling to a man whose only sin was that he was fool enough to love her."

His voice was like a whip-lash and Nevada stared at him incredulously.

"Now I understand why you are incensed with me," she said, "but surely it is rather ridiculous? After

all, I did not ask David to fall in love with me, or
Charles for that matter."

"You only made quite certain they would," Tyrone Strome said, "and you were quite prepared, Nevada, to try your wiles on me."

He laughed.

"Unfortunately, as far as I was concerned you
were just not clever enough. In fact, for a woman of
even limited experience it was a lamentable performance."

She felt that his scorn was more insulting than if
he had been angry.

"I want something to eat," she said sullenly.

"Of course, and there is plenty of food aboard the
yacht," Tyrone Strome replied. "But if you want to
eat, then you must get it for yourself. You know where
the Galley is, I presume?"

She looked at him uncertainly.

"Why cannot a steward . . . bring it to me?"

"Because I think it would be good for you to look
after yourself; to find for the first time in your life that
your money cannot buy you everything."

"This is ridiculous!"

"You may think so, but I would point out to you
that this is my yacht and I run it as I wish to do. If
you are hungry you get yourself something to eat, or
go without. Incidentally, there will be no-one to wait
on you in your cabin."

"How dare you treat me like this!"

"It is not very difficult," Tyrone Strome retorted.
"Perhaps it will teach you not to travel about the world
another time without ensuring you are adequately
protected. I dislike the idea of a woman thinking she
does not need protection."

"I certainly have no wish to be protected by you!"
Nevada said rudely.

As she spoke she realised her mistake, for the
smile on Tyrone Strome's face was merely that of a
man coping with a fractious child or an obstreperous
animal.

She got to her feet.

"Where is this Galley?" she demanded.

"Aft, as is usual," he answered. "As it is nearly luncheon-time, you will find the Chef there. He is Chinese, so you will not be able to communicate with him."

Because she felt she would get no further by arguing, Nevada walked out of the Saloon and slammed the door behind her.

When without difficulty she found the Galley in the stern of the ship she realised it was a very modern and up-to-date one, far better in fact than any Galley she had seen before.

The Chinese Chef, assisted by a younger man, both in spotless white clothes, were preparing luncheon and the fragrance of the food made Nevada realise how very hungry she was.

Knowing she could not converse with the Chef, she told him in sign-language that she was hungry and he pointed to a stool on the other side of the narrow table at which he was working.

The stove was behind him and on it Nevada saw that he was grilling a steak.

Although the sea was calm, it was easier to sit than stand, so she took the stool and sat watching the Chef as he deftly prepared the garnishing for the meal—small fresh mushrooms, aubergines, and tiny spring peas.

On the side of the stove Nevada saw a dish of asparagus, which had been one of her favourite dishes at the Villa, since it came fresh to the market every day from the fields behind Nice.

The steak was ready and the Chef lifted it from the stove onto a dish. The garnishings were set round it and almost as if he had been called a steward appeared, also wearing a spotless white coat, although he sported gold buttons.

He carried a tray with a cloth on it neatly laid with shining silver.

As he set it down on the table the assistant to the Chef placed the dish of asparagus and an already mixed salad on it with two sauce boats while the Chef covered the steak with a silver cover and placed it on a hot plate on the tray.

Then to Nevada's consternation the steward turned and walked out of the Galley.

It was only then that she realised the tray was intended for Tyrone Strome and had in fact been laid only for one.

"What about me?" she cried to the Chef, pointing to herself as she did so.

In answer he took another steak which was raw and uncooked and set it down in front of her. He pushed what remained of the mushrooms, peas, and aubergines, also in their natural state, towards her and he and his assistant left the Galley.

For a moment Nevada could hardly realise what had happened. Then she knew they were obeying orders and, as Tyrone Strome had said, she had to look after herself.

For a moment she clenched her small hands in fury and wanted to throw the steak to the floor and stamp on it.

Then an aching void inside her told her that she was extremely, unashamedly hungry and anger would get her nowhere.

Tentatively she rose to her feet and going round to the other side of the table she picked up the steak gingerly with her thumb and forefinger and dropped it onto the grill.

* * *

Tyrone Strome came from the bridge where he had been discussing with the Captain the progress they had made during the day and entered the Saloon.

The yacht was certainly living up to her reputation as one of the fastest vessels of her kind afloat.

The reason he had built her to his own specifications was simply that there were times in his life when he wished to get away with all possible speed from a situation which had become too explosive to be healthy.

The *Moulay* had never failed in an emergency.

His crew had all been with him for a long time, and he knew they would obey any order he gave them without question and with an implicit obedience that he found admirable.

He could not help wondering as he walked along the deck towards the Saloon how Nevada had enjoyed the first meal he was sure she had ever cooked for herself.

It had been reported to him exactly what had happened, and he thought with a ruthless expression on his face that the easiest way to learn how to cook was to go hungry if one did not do so.

He was wondering too how Nevada without maids was managing in her cabin.

He was sure that as a millionairess she had never so much as picked up a piece of paper from the floor.

She was the type of parasite he most disliked.

Self-made millionaires at least had worked hard for their money, but their pampered, cossetted women who believed that money could buy everything in the wide world had always aroused his scorn.

He thought that Nevada would find life aboard the *Moulay* very different from that which she had enjoyed in her father's house on Fifth Avenue and his great estates in other parts of America.

Tyrone Strome entered the Saloon intent on getting back to his desk. He had just settled himself and was turning over the papers on which he had been working when the door opened and Nevada came in.

She was wearing the same white gown she had worn earlier in the day but there was a glint in her eyes that had not been there before and he had a feeling she was up to some mischief.

"What is it?" he asked coldly. "I am in fact rather busy."

"I think you have time to listen to me," Nevada replied.

He had made no effort to rise at her appearance and now he said impatiently:

"As it happens, Nevada, I have a lot of work to

do and I really must excuse myself from further arguments. You had better be sporting enough to make the best of a bad job."

"I am sporting enough to be quite a good shot!" Nevada answered.

As she spoke she drew from behind the full skirts of her gown a revolver and pointed it at Tyrone Strome.

He did not start, he merely looked at her as if he waited for an explanation.

"You will send for the Captain," Nevada said, "and tell him to turn the yacht back and take me to the nearest port."

"And if I refuse?"

"Then you will find yourself in considerable pain."

There was a note of triumph in her voice as she went on:

"I shall not kill you, as I have no wish to be tried for murder. Also, as you well know, I cannot give orders to your crew. But I will shoot you in the arm, which you will find very painful, and if you still do not obey me I shall shoot you in the leg."

"You have thought it out very carefully," Tyrone Strome remarked.

"As you see, I am capable of looking after myself," Nevada replied, "and to make sure that I could do so in any situation like this I have practised shooting on my father's ranch in Colorado."

Tyrone Strome did not reply and she added:

"Come on now . . . you are defeated and you know it! Send for the Captain or I promise you my threat will become reality."

"As I do not wish him to leave the bridge," Tyrone Strome replied, "I will write him a note."

He pulled a piece of paper towards him with his left hand and picked up his pen to dip it into the large, square-based ink-pot which stood on the desk.

Nevada watched him with a smile on her lips.

Suddenly as his hand holding the pen moved,

Tyrone Strome struck the ink-pot violently so that it shot off the desk and straight towards her.

Instinctively as any woman would have done she stepped back to prevent the ink from spoiling her gown and as she did so Tyrone Strome with the incredible swiftness of a trained athlete sprang over the desk and seized her arm to fling it upwards.

She gave a cry of sheer fury. But almost before it had left her lips, before even she could pull the trigger of the revolver, he had taken it from her and had put the weapon in his pocket.

She stood staring at him furiously, a pool of ink between them on the floor.

Then as if his action snapped the last vestige of her self-control she rushed at him, her fingers pointed, clawing at his face.

He held her away from him with one hand and slapped her hard against the cheek with the other.

The sound was like a pistol-shot and it not only checked Nevada's assault but swept away her fury, so that she stood staring at him in astonishment, her fingers going up to her cheek.

"You hit me!"

Her voice was not angry but merely surprised.

"Yes, I hit you," Tyrone Strome answered, "and I shall hit you again if you behave like a fish-wife. In a physical battle, Nevada, you must be intelligent enough to know that you have no chance of winning."

She stood looking at him, her hand still on her burning cheek. Then with a sound that was curiously like a sob she turned and ran from the Saloon.

✿ ✿ ✿

For what was left of the day Nevada lay on her bunk planning how she could get even with Tyrone Strome.

She had been so confident, when she remembered the revolver in her trunk, that she would be able to force him into taking her to the nearest port.

She had plenty of money besides jewellery that

was worth a small fortune, and she was quite certain that wherever she was put ashore she could find her way back to Europe and eventually to America.

But Tyrone Strome had defeated her.

While she hated him for doing so, she could not help feeling there were few men who had his strength and agility.

"I loathe him!" she said aloud. "He shall not treat me like this! I will kill him rather than let him win!"

It was easy to say, but impossible to do without a weapon.

The small revolver with which she always travelled and which had given her a sense of security was now in Tyrone Strome's possession and she had nothing else with which she could threaten him.

She thought of throwing herself overboard merely to annoy him. Then she had the uncomfortable feeling that perhaps he would consider it a good way to be rid of her and make little attempt to go to her rescue.

She could not really believe that he would let her drown. At the same time, she had begun to realise there was a ruthlessness about him she had never encountered before.

"I have to defeat him . . . I have to!" she told herself all through the night.

But when the morning came it was impossible to stay in her cabin and starve.

She went to the Galley eventually, only to find that apparently everyone else had breakfasted and the Chef had gone.

There were some eggs and rashers of bacon lying on the table and with the greatest difficulty Nevada managed to cook them.

Her only experience of cooking had been at the barbecues she had sometimes attended in the country when her friends had thought it amusing to cook steaks and sausages on an open charcoal fire and she had allowed the better-looking male guests to wait on her.

She burnt her fingers, and the food when she had

cooked it was, she thought, almost inedible. But because she was so hungry she ate it, although the main part of her breakfast consisted of bread and butter.

There appeared to be no jam or honey and she wondered where they were kept, but as there was no-one to ask she had to content herself with what she could find.

When she went back to her cabin it was exactly as she had left it. The bed was crumpled after she had slept in it, the clothes that she had discarded yesterday were still lying on the floor.

She kicked her gown in exasperation; then, knowing it was one of her prettiest, she picked it up and hung it in the wardrobe.

She looked at her large collection of trunks with dislike.

How could she possibly cope with all this luggage by herself? And after she had unpacked the things she wanted to wear, how was she going to pack them again?

She sat down on her bunk and tried to think what she could do and how she could persuade Tyrone Strome, if not by force then by other means, to stop this quite absurd punishment.

That was what it was, Nevada knew, a punishment because he thought she had been unkind to his nephew, David.

"I always knew men stuck together," she told herself, "but this is past all bearing."

She thought that she disliked not only Tyrone Strome but David and every other young man like him. In fact she hated all men and in the future she would take every possible opportunity to hurt them and make them suffer.

But this did not help the position she was in at the moment: she was in Tyrone Strome's power and could see no way out of it.

Then, after thinking for a long time, she decided she must use a different sort of tactic.

Pulling her things out of one of the big trunks until she found a gown that she thought made her look very young and rather wistful, she arranged her hair in a different style and went to the Saloon.

As she expected, Tyrone Strome was at his desk.

"Are you . . . very busy?" she asked in a soft, hesitating voice. "If you are . . . I could come back later."

"What do you want?" he asked uncompromisingly.

"I want . . . to talk to you."

"There is nothing to discuss."

"It would be very . . . kind and only fair if you would . . . listen to what I have to say."

With what she thought was an exasperated sigh he pushed his papers aside and said:

"Very well! If you are going to throw a bomb at me, or if you have a javelin hidden in your petticoats, get it over. I am busy!"

"It is . . . nothing like that."

Nevada walked to the desk and sat down on the edge of the chair facing him.

Her eyes were very large and green, and her red hair, which she had arranged so skilfully, framed her heart-shaped face like a halo.

"What I want to say to you . . . Mr. Strome," she said, "is simply that I am . . . sorry."

Tyrone Strome's eyes were on her face as she continued:

"I have been . . . thinking over what you said and I realise now that I was . . . wrong . . . completely and absolutely wrong to be so . . . unkind to David. I did not . . . think that he was . . . serious in threatening to take his life . . . in fact I can only tell you that I am very . . . ignorant about . . . men . . . having been an . . . only child."

Her eyes dropped and her lashes were very dark against her white skin as Nevada went on in a low voice:

"I am sorry . . . really sorry that I should have been . . . so unkind."

She waited for Tyrone Strome's reply, then he laughed.

"An excellent threatrical performance, Nevada. It is a pity you are so rich. You could have made your fortune on the stage!"

"I am not . . . play-acting," she protested, but despite herself her voice rose a little.

"All you need now is an appreciative audience," he said. "I am quite certain if it had been a female one you would have had them in tears. As it is, I am afraid I am very sceptical of penitants who retract at the sight of the rack!"

Nevada's lips tightened for a moment.

He was driving her very hard and it was difficult for her to keep her temper.

"You must believe me . . . Mr. Strome," she said. "I really am . . . sorry."

"Then I am delighted to hear it, but that does not mean that I shall change my plans or alter my intentions of turning you into a woman. I hope you will enjoy your luncheon, and now you must excuse me if I continue with my work."

Nevada rose to her feet.

"Please do not go on with this," she pleaded, and now she was not acting. "Take me back . . . I promise you that I will never communicate with David or your sister ever again . . . but I cannot stay here . . . like this."

"Why not?" Tyrone Strome asked.

"Because I have never . . . lived like this before."

"Then you will doubtless find it an adventure, something which it might amuse you to relate to your friends when you return to New York."

"When may I go home?"

"When I consider you are ready to do so."

"Do be serious," Nevada begged. "You have had your revenge. I am prepared to grovel and say that I am sorry, to apologise for everything, but I cannot stay here alone with you. If anyone should hear of it they would be very shocked."

"No-one will hear of it," Tyrone Strome replied, "I have taken good care of that. David, Charles, and everyone else, with the exception of my sister, be-

lieve you have returned to America. When Mrs.
Langholme writes to ask if she may join you, my sister will deal with the situation. After all, there are a
great number of people in the South of France and
elsewhere who might wish you to be their guest."

Nevada drew in her breath. She felt as if he im-
prisoned her in a dungeon from which there was no
escape.

"As for scandal," Tyrone Strome went on, "if you
talk of what has occurred on this journey when you
return to civilisation, that is entirely up to you."

"Do you suppose I would want to talk about it?"
Nevada demanded angrily. "You are making a fool of
me, as you well know. You are treating me as if I
were a delinquent. That is certainly nothing to be
proud of. Why go on with it? You have had your
revenge. Is that not enough?"

"I told you that we all have ambitions of some
sort or another," Tyrone Strome answered, "and mine
at the moment is to turn a very unpleasant young
specimen of humanity into something different. I may
fail. It may prove impossible, but at least I shall have
tried."

"I am not unpleasant," Nevada stormed, "nor am
I bad and evil as you are trying to make out. I have
been thoughtless, I am prepared to admit that my
head has been turned by so much admiration, but
otherwise I am just an ordinary girl with feelings like
everyone else."

"On the contrary, I should say that you are very
unordinary," Tyrone said. "For instance, you have
told me that you dislike the thought of love."

"That certainly is true," Nevada remarked.

"What other woman with your assets could have
no softness, no sympathy or compassion for the men
who fall in love with her?" Tyrone asked. "And who
would not wish to love and be loved, as men and
women have done since the beginning of time?"

His voice seemed to ring out round the Saloon.

"Can I help the way I am?" Nevada snapped.

"That is what I am going to find out," Tyrone

Strome replied. "It may take quite a long time, so the sooner you get used to the idea the better!"

Nevada stamped her foot.

"I hate you! I hate and loathe you! If I get a chance to kill you I will do so. If I had had any sense I would have shot you before you took my revolver away from me."

"What a pity you did not think of that sooner," Tyrone Strome replied mockingly.

Nevada's hands were clenched and he knew that she was longing to fly at him again and scratch his face as she had tried to do before.

Then, as if she remembered how he had slapped her, she turned and rushed out of the Saloon, once again slamming the door behind her.

Tyrone Strome laughed and picked up his papers.

Chapter Four

Swaying on top of a camel, Nevada thought, was rather like being on top of the waves.

She could hardly imagine that what was happening to her was true and she was in fact travelling in a sort of sedan-chair on a camel's back. It was made of braided and coloured wicker and had a curtained awning above her head.

She was aware that this litter was used only by the women of the highest Saharan society and that the others had to walk draped in blue veils or in Moslem fashion covered completely by a *haik*.

She had learnt the name of this tent-like white garment from the books she had read before she left the yacht.

But they had not prepared her for her sensational departure from it when it seemed to her she lost her own identity and became a chattel of Tyrone Strome.

As the yacht had moved along the coast of Morocco she had lowered her pride sufficiently to ask him if she could have some books to read.

She had grown very bored with either sulking in her cabin, which seemed to grow smaller and more uncomfortable with every trunk she opened, or else walking alone on deck ignored by both her host and the members of his crew.

The only break in the monotony of the days was when she had to cook herself something to eat.

It was almost an agony to see the succulent and delicious dishes that were prepared for Tyrone Strome and then to be left with pieces of raw meat, chicken, or fish, which she must prepare for herself.

"I loathe cooking!" Nevada said over and over again.

Nevertheless, she watched the Chinese Chef at work and after a little while she found that the food she cooked was not quite as unpalatable as it had been at first.

The humiliation of having to go to the Galley for anything she ate hurt her pride, as, she told herself, did everything else aboard the *Moulay*.

Then this morning when after breakfast she was standing in the sunshine on deck looking at the coastline, to her surprise Tyrone Strome had joined her.

He stood at the railing also looking towards the shore, and although she told herself she would not speak first, something about him seemed to force her into asking:

"Where are we?"

"The last place we passed," he replied, "was Agadir. That of course is where the High Atlas Mountains meet the sea."

Nevada was not going to admit it but she had in fact been tremendously impressed by the great dry brown elephantine peaks towering above the turbulent blue of the Atlantic.

There had been gigantic spray-lashed cliffs alternating with verdant valleys which were planted, she thought, with banana trees and maize.

Then there had been a half-moon bay lined with peach-coloured sand behind which there was the flat-topped roofs of a town which she had thought was Agadir.

It nestled in a green valley surrounded by trees and she thought how beautiful it was and she wished she could talk to someone about it.

But she had no intention of breaking her almost monosyllabic silence where Tyrone Strome was concerned.

She hated him even more ferociously than she had done the first days of the voyage.

In fact the only time her thoughts veered from loathing the man who was punishing her was when she lost herself in the books which he lent her.

There were quite a number of book-cases which she had not noticed previously in the Saloon and nearly all the books she had found were about Africa and in particular Morocco.

The majority were written in French and she was thankful that her education, on which her father had expended a small fortune, enabled her to read that language with ease.

At first she had thought there was nothing in the book-case to interest her, but after she had begun to read a little about the history of Morocco she wanted to know more.

She discovered that even the warfare between the different tribes was fascinating, and because she was a quick reader she found herself changing her books not once but several times a day.

Because she wished to avoid Tyrone Strome, she usually went to the Saloon when she knew he was either on the bridge or exercising himself on deck.

He not only walked an enormous amount, but he also, she found, did gymnastic exercises, which would account for his athletic agility.

She had not forgotten—and even to think of it made her cheeks burn with anger—how he had taken her revolver from her when she had thought she had him in her power.

There had been silence after Tyrone Strome had told her they had passed Agadir. Then because she could not repress her curiosity Nevada enquired:

"Where are we going?"

"I was just going to speak to you about that."

He leaned on the railing as he spoke, looking out towards the coastline, and glancing at him without turning her head Nevada thought that he not only looked infuriatingly handsome, but also that he had something unpleasant to tell her.

"In a short time we are leaving the yacht," he said, "and because we will be travelling in a part of the world that sees few if any Europeans, you will dress as a Berber woman and wear a *litham*."

This was the Arabic word, Nevada knew from her reading, for what most Europeans and Americans called a "yashmak."

"I refuse!" she said promptly.

She was actually intrigued by the idea of exploring new territory, but she had no intention of admitting any interest in Tyrone Strome's nefarious schemes and she was determined to oppose him in every way in her power.

"I have already explained," he said quietly as if speaking to a child, "that it would be unwise and perhaps dangerous for us to go where I am taking you unless we follow the customs of the country."

"As I have no wish to go anywhere with you, Mr. Strome," Nevada replied, "I shall wear what I wish to wear. If you do not like it, the obvious remedy is to return me to Europe and stop behaving like a barbarian."

"If I were a barbarian," Tyrone Strome replied, "you might have a very different complaint about the treatment you have received during the time you have been alone with me aboard my yacht."

For a moment she looked a him wide-eyed. Then when she saw the expression on his face and the mocking twist to his lips she looked away quickly, aware that her heart had given a start that was unmistakably one of fear.

"Go and dress yourself in the clothes you will find in your cabin," he said, "and that is an order!"

Because she felt she would not let herself be down-trodden, because she would assert herself even though it was difficult to do so, Nevada replied, lifting her chin:

"And if I refuse?"

"You will find I am a very competent lady's-maid," Tyrone Strome answered slowly, almost drawling the words, "and I have in fact had quite a lot of experience!"

There was no doubt now of the innuendo behind the words, and the colour in Nevada's cheeks flared crimson as she turned and went below, her whole body shaking as she did so with anger.

She went into her cabin to stare about her in astonishment, for all her trunks had disappeared.

Everything had gone except a small native-style wicker basket in which she saw there was one of her nightgowns and a plain brush and comb which did not belong to her.

On the dressing-table the gold fittings of her dressing-case had vanished and instead there were a number of small bottles and tiny boxes which she found contained native cosmetics.

There was khol, with which Eastern women outlined their eyes; there was henna, which she knew was to redden the palms of her hands and the soles of her feet; and there was a coloured salve for her lips.

She stared at them in surprise, then turned to see laid out on the bed a white caftan exquisitely embroidered with gold thread, a double-veiled *litham,* and beside it a white *haik.*

This tent-like garment worn by Moslem women was, she knew, a disguise in which she would be completely unidentifiable.

Also on the bed there was some gold jewellery: necklaces, long drop ear-rings, bangles, and what Nevada thought must be a head-piece.

It had a large ornamental jewelled plaque in the centre of the forehead with a turquoise drop falling from it surrounded by small diamonds.

Her own jewellery and, more important, all the money she possessed had gone and for the moment she contemplated storming up on deck to accuse Tyrone Strome of being a thief as well as everything else.

Then she told herself he would only ignore her protestations.

Moreover, she had the uncomfortable feeling that he had not been joking when he said that if she did not obey him and put on the clothes he had provided, he would undress her himself.

"How could this be happening to me?" Nevada asked aloud.

Then because she was in fact afraid, although she would not admit it, she slowly undressed and put on the caftan.

She was not sure what she should do about her hair; she felt certain it would look absurd arranged in a fashionable style as she usually wore it.

So she took out the pins and let it fall over her shoulders.

As she looked at herself in the mirror she could not help thinking that the fiery red of it, which reached nearly to her waist, was offset to advantage by the white and gold caftan.

Then she asked herself almost plaintively, "What is the point of looking attractive for a man who hates me as violently as I hate him?"

But time was passing and she put on the ornate head-dress, arranging the turquoise drop in the centre of her forehead. Then with an expression of distaste she picked up the *litham*.

She held it in her hands, feeling that it signified her complete capitulation to the authority and will of Tyrone Strome, when there was a knock at the door.

Without waiting for her reply he came into the cabin.

"Are you ready yet?"

"I have no idea how to arrange this," she replied, holding out the *litham* towards him.

He took it from her, looking as he did so at her red hair falling over her shoulders.

"Put on the ear-rings first."

She picked them up from the bed and set them in her ears.

Because amongst her mother's jewellery there

were ear-rings that were exceedingly valuable, Nevada's ears were pierced.

The long gold ornately worked rings hung easily from her small lobes, but she thought that by the end of the day they would feel very heavy.

There were a number of bracelets for her wrists and rings for her fingers.

"Henna your hands," Tyrone Strome ordered, "and also colour your nails!"

She wanted to defy him and refuse, but somehow in the smallness of the cabin he seemed so large and overpowering that almost automatically she obeyed.

It took her a little time and he stood beside her, saying nothing but making her acutely conscious of his presence.

When she had finished and her hands looked very different from the way she was used to seeing them, he said:

"Now outline your eyes with khol!"

Again Nevada longed to refuse, but she knew it was useless. With the black line her eyes looked enormous and very green.

Tyrone Strome picked up the *litham* and arranged it over her nose. There was something indifferent about the touch of his hands.

'I might be a puppet or a piece of wood,' Nevada thought crossly.

He then took the *haik* from the bed and waited for her to rise from the chair on which she was sitting. He covered her with the all-enveloping garment, then turned towards the door.

"We shall be going ashore in ten minutes. A steward will show you up on deck where I shall be waiting for you. You will not speak to me but will follow where I lead you until we reach the camels."

As he finished speaking he left the cabin.

As if her legs felt too weak to support her, Nevada sat down again on a chair and looked at herself in the mirror.

Could this bundle of a woman with only two eyes to identify her really be herself?

She had the terrifying feeling that she was leaving Nevada Van Arden behind and that she would be lost completely, never to reappear in the world she had known before.

Then she told herself she was being imaginative and that if nothing else this was an adventure which would be amusing someday to relate and perhaps to write down in her diary.

When a steward came to collect her and the wicker basket, she walked proudly ahead of him up on deck, determined that if she was afraid Tyrone Strome should not be aware of it.

Then when she saw him it was in fact with a start of astonishment, for she had forgotten that if she was to be dressed as a native so was he.

He was all in white, wearing the magnificent flowing garments of a Sheik. His *serwal,* or trousers, ended with tapering legs hugging his calves above red leather riding-boots.

His head was covered with a white turban which she knew would be worn by the more important Berber Chieftains.

Strapped to his left side with a silk cord was a Moorish dagger in a jewel-studded sheath.

If she had not hated him so violently Nevada would have admitted that the flowing robes made Tyrone Strome seem even taller and more imposing than he appeared in European dress.

His skin was very sunburnt and his fine-cut features made it quite easy to credit that he was in fact from one of the ancient tribes with which Southern Morocco abounded.

He did not speak to her, but the moment she appeared he turned and walked down the gang-plank onto what she saw was a small jetty against which the yacht was moored.

It was not, she was sure, a regular port; in fact beyond the jetty there were very few buildings.

Those there were seemed small and dilapidated, constructed only of the same hard-baked soil on which they were erected.

However, as soon as she stepped ashore Nevada had eyes not for the buildings or even for the desert-like surroundings where they were disembarking.

Instead she saw only the camels and the donkeys which were waiting for them, realising that in fact it was what constituted a caravan.

The camels were sitting down, turning their long serpent-like necks first one way and then another, and making a strange noise that sounded like a strangled growl or a curious bubbling.

Tyrone Strome was being greeted by men wearing light blue cotton robes and black turbans.

They were tall, graceful, and muscular, with long black silky hair, black eyes, small noses, and, Nevada noticed, curiously delicate hands.

She guessed, and longed to ask if she was right, that they were the so-called "Blue Men," southern Morocco's legendary desert nomads, men of Arabic and Berber descent mainly from the Regeibat tribes.

Their nickname came from their blue-dyed clothing, since the dyes were not fast and sometimes their bodies and faces also became blue-stained.

Despite her resolution to oppose Tyrone Strome in every possible way, to show if not hostility then complete indifference to anything he did, Nevada could not help being interested in the Blue Men and their camels.

The animals' saddles were decorated with fringes ornamented with amber, with tassels and coloured stones which Nevada felt must be pieces of porcelain, but she was not sure.

She had little time to look round her as Tyrone Strome with a wave of his hand indicated a camel which had on its back a litter in which she realised she was to travel.

One of the Blue Men helped her into it, keeping his eyes averted from her face although there was nothing to see but her eyes.

Then as Nevada held on tightly to the arms of her strange chair, the camel rose awkwardly to his feet and they set off in a long procession.

It was led by Tyrone Strome on a horse, followed by men riding donkeys or leading camels laden with what appeared to be luggage or packages.

Nevada found it extremely tantalising that she had no idea where they were going, and she wished now that she had asked Tyrone Strome more questions when he first told her they were leaving the yacht.

It was obvious that where they were was almost desert, except there was a lack of sand.

It was in fact a flat stony waste-land, mile upon mile of gravel-strewn country without vegetation.

But it had in itself a strange beauty because the soil could change its hue from dead grey to orange-brass and copper-brown to pure ochre.

She was conscious of measureless space and a tremendous overarching sky above.

They must have travelled for nearly two hours, finding little variation in the desert-like scenery except that occasionally in the distance Nevada would see a building and knew it was a Kasbah.

They were small and she was sure they were not important, but because they were built from the soil on which they stood they varied in colour.

One she noticed was the creamy brown of café-au-lait and she saw that round it were some palms and fruit trees.

But Tyrone Strome obviously had no intention of stopping and they moved on, slowly, relentlessly, Nevada swaying with every step, and she was only thankful the movement did not make her sea-sick.

Suddenly, unexpectedly, Tyrone Strome held up his hand and the caravan came to a halt.

Nevada was surprised.

There was no change in the scenery and they seemed to have reached nowhere.

Turning his horse's head, Tyrone Strome rode back down the line of camels and donkeys until he reached Nevada.

He gave a sharp order in Arabic; the man who was leading her camel spoke, and the animal slowly, grunting as he did, went down on his knees.

Nevada looked enquiringly at Tyrone Strome.

"Get down," he ordered.

Wonderingly, glad for the moment to be free of the swaying litter, Nevada, helped by the camel-driver, stepped onto the sand.

She was wearing *babouches* decorated with gold embroidery. They were very light slippers and the stones hurt the soles of her feet.

As she moved forward tentatively, hoping she would not have to walk far, Tyrone Strome swung himself off his horse and came to her side.

"I have something to show you."

She looked at him in surprise. There appeared to be nothing on either side of them.

Then he led her a little way from the caravan to where she saw what appeared to be a heap on the ground.

As they drew nearer, Nevada, thinking of little but the discomfort to her feet, saw large white bones, then a skull.

Tyrone Strome stopped.

"You thought it would be interesting to see a dead man," he said. "Well, here is one. He was murdered, and Moorish custom prohibits the burial of a victim until after vengeance has been taken on his murderer."

Nevada gave a little gasp.

Now she could see the skeleton lying full length where he had fallen. The vultures had plucked the flesh from his bones so that his lipless teeth seemed to grin in his skull with its empty eye-sockets.

There were his finger-bones lying by what had at one time been his body, and the sun, or perhaps the vultures which had devoured him, had left only the rags of his *djellaba* and turban.

She gave a little gasp and would have turned away, but Tyrone Strome reached out and caught hold of her wrist

"I want you to look at this man," he said, his voice hard and contemptuous. "Think of him as he was, young and virile, optimistic, perhaps ambitious, and very probably in love."

He pulled Nevada a little closer as he said:

"Now he is dead, look at what is left of him."

"Let me . . . go!"

She tried to pull herself from his clasp but realized how helpless she was.

"You find the idea of death amusing," Tyrone Strome went on. "To me it is a pitiable waste when it comes too soon! A waste that a young man must die because of the greed of an assailant or the cruelty of a woman."

Nevada shut her eyes.

She could not bear to look at the skeleton. She felt as if Tyrone Strome's condemnation was as horrible as the fleshless bones and the empty sockets where eyes had once looked at life with curiosity.

Suddenly she felt she would faint. She must have swayed a little, so Tyrone Strome was aware of what was happening.

His hands released her wrist and because Nevada felt she could bear no more she turned and stumbled blindly back towards the camels.

Somehow she was helped onto the litter and when they started off again, Tyrone Strome leading the way, she put her hands up to her eyes and covered her face.

Had she really mocked at death? Had she really incited David to take his life?

It all seemed to have happened a long time ago; yet, if he had died, she knew now she would never have been able to forgive herself . . . or forget.

They moved on for another hour. Then reaching a cluster of palm trees the caravan once again came to a halt.

As she dismounted, Nevada realised they had reached an oasis, and because the sun had been hot she was thankful for the cool shade of the feathery branches.

She had found that the veil over her face was extremely heating and she longed to set it on one side.

Only her fear of Tyrone Strome's reaction prevented her from doing so.

She saw that one of the camel-drivers had taken a brightly coloured rug from his camel and had set it down at the far end of the oasis. As Tyrone Strome walked towards it she realised that that was where he would sit.

She waited, wondering where she was to go, when he turned and beckoned to her.

She walked towards him, feeling more eager than she might otherwise have been because she was thirsty.

At least, she thought, here in the middle of the desert she would not be expected to cook her own meal.

Tyrone Strome sat down on the rug.

His legs were crossed under him in the conventional attitude of the East. Nevada wanted to copy him but she found that owing to the narrowness of her caftan she could only kneel and sit back on her heels.

Food was set in front of them and a servant carried a goat-skin which Nevada knew contained water.

It was poured into a glass, and while she longed to drink it immediately she had the feeling that to remove her veil while a servant was there would be incorrect and so she waited.

At last the men who were attending to them moved away and Nevada noticed that although the camel-drivers and other attendants sat at the other side of the oasis they all turned their backs out of respect for their master's privacy.

"Now you may drink," Tyrone Strome said.

Thankfully Nevada pushed aside her veil and drank off the whole glass of water without a pause.

It tasted slightly brackish but at that moment she would have welcomed anything that was liquid.

"You are all right?"

It was the first time he had shown the slightest concern for her. She thought he was not only thinking of her reaction to the corpse, but that he had expected her to feel sick from the method by which she was travelling.

"I am all right," she answered. "Where are we going?"

"We are staying tonight at a Kasbah belonging to one of the most important Sheiks in South Morocco. It may not be very comfortable for you, because you will be in the women's quarters."

Nevada looked at him wide-eyed.

"Do you mean . . . the Harem?"

"A Harem in Morocco does not have exactly the same meaning as one in Turkey," Tyrone Strome replied, "but I do not suppose you would notice the difference."

Nevada was silent.

She felt suddenly more afraid than she had ever been before. There was something frightening about going to a strange place of which she knew nothing and where she would be of no importance save that she belonged to Tyrone Strome.

As if he knew what she was feeling he said:

"We are staying for only one night, but it is important for me not only to meet the Sheik Hassam El Zigli, with whom we will be staying, but other Sheiks and *Caids* of the neighbourhood."

"Why should you want to meet them?" Nevada enquired.

She wondered if he would give her a truthful answer or if it had something to do with his secret exploits.

To her surprise, Tyrone Strome replied:

"I am writing a book."

"A book!"

It was somehow the last thing she had expected him to say.

"Does it surprise you?" he asked. "Morocco has always been a country of mystery: very little is known about it and less still about the people who inhabit it."

Nevada's eyes were on his.

She was interested despite herself—extremely interested—and she was frightened in case he should
stop telling her what she wished to know.

"About eighty-six per cent of the Moroccan pop-
ulation is Berber or Arab," Tyrone Strome said, "and
the Berbers are the magnificent, age-old mysterious
backbone of North Africa."

He smiled as if at the romanticism of his words
before he went on:

"They are a Mediterranean people and not at all
Negroid, nor are they Semitic. In fact, where they
come from God only knows."

"And you are writing about them?"

"It is very difficult to find out all I need for a
book. They have lived in North Africa, especially
among the mountains, since the dawn of time. The
Pharaohs of Egypt, mystified by them, called them
Lebu; the Greeks, who were equally mystified called
them Nomades. No-one even knows where the word
'Berber' comes from."

"And you like them?"

"They are a people whom I find fascinating,"
Tyrone Strome replied, "and they are completely un-
spoilt by civilisation."

He laughed.

"Where else in the world today will you find
slavery taken as a matter of course, men who are prepared to live by the sword and dagger, and women
are pure and obedient?"

The last two words held an innuendo which told
Nevada that he was mocking at her, but for once she
was not annoyed.

"Tell me more," she begged.

"You will find that this world is worth studying,
worth exploring," he answered. "But if we are to arrive at our destination as early as I intend, I suggest
that you eat quickly."

Because she was extremely hungry Nevada
obeyed him and they finished their meal in silence.

She had the feeling as she did so that this was the

last European food she might eat for a long time and she wondered what lay ahead.

As soon as they were finished they set out once more and now the surroundings seemed to alter, and the ground became more rocky and rough.

Suddenly ahead of them Nevada saw what seemed to her to be an enormous fortified town.

She stared at it in astonishment for it was of colossal construction, surrounded by ramparts of various heights and sizes.

It topped a slight elevation and the buildings were all bristling with very high crenellated ramparts from which here and there massive towers protruded.

As Tyrone Strome led the caravan nearer it seemed even bigger and more impressive and hastily Nevada tried to remember what she had learnt about the Kasbahs in the books she had read on the yacht.

Somewhere she had learnt that they were like large mediaeval Castles, being occupied by the Chieftain of the Tribe together with all his followers, servants, and anyone who owed him allegiance.

Besides human beings, his animals, cows, goats, sheep, donkeys, mules, and chickens also sheltered in the Kasbah, as was their right.

In the daytime all the beasts would be driven out either to work or to fend for themselves, but at night they returned through the main gate to stay safe and protected until dawn.

The Kasbah was not therefore just a habitation but a little principality, a self-sufficient domain that provided most of the things necessary for daily life except tea, coffee, and sugar.

Tyrone Strome had now reached an enormous wooden brass-studded door. It was open and a number of white-robed men came running out to welcome him.

They led everyone inside and now Nevada could see a whole succession of twisting galleries off which she had an occasional glimpse of court-yards and fountains.

Still on her camel, she was carried through a labyrinth of twisting passages filled with men, children, and animals, until finally she reached what she guessed was the centre of the Kasbah where the Sheik himself lived.

Here, she realised as she dismounted, everything was very different.

She followed Tyrone Strome through an elaborately carved door and found herself in what she could only describe as a Palace.

Looking at the austere, windowless, gaunt outside of the Kasbah, it was strange to find that inside there were floors of the finest mosaic and walls covered either with carved arabesques or tiles of intricate patterns in many colours.

The ceilings were of carved wood and richly painted, columns with carved capitals separated some of the rooms, and there were screens of lattice-work that were very lovely.

Multicoloured High Atlas rugs covered the floors and Nevada saw silk-embroidered hassocks of red, green, white, and yellow leather made from goatskin.

Silver lanterns were suspended from the ceilings and she thought as she glanced around that the whole place seemed mysterious and Eastern in a way she could not describe.

Sheik Hassam El Zigli, an elderly man with a white beard, wearing in his belt a jewelled dagger covered in precious stones, came hurrying forward to greet Tyrone Strome with every mark of respect.

He ignored Nevada standing a little behind him, and only after the men had talked together for some moments did Tyrone Strome apparently mention her presence.

The Sheik snapped his fingers.

A servant appeared and beckoned Nevada to follow him.

She felt suddenly afraid of leaving Tyrone Strome and disappearing into this huge labyrinth that seemed to be half Palace and half slum.

Then she told herself he would despise her more than he did already if she showed any fear.

Without looking at him she followed the servant, and once again they were moving through long twisting passages for what seemed to Nevada to be a very long way.

Finally there was another impressive door, carved and ornamented in Moorish fashion, and the servant knocked.

It was opened by a veiled woman who, although Nevada could not understand what was said, was obviously told who she was.

The woman beckoned her in, the door was shut behind her, and she felt more alone than she had ever felt in her whole life.

The woman spoke to her but she could only shake her head. Then she was led through another passage and finally into a large room in which there were a number of women.

They were unveiled, and were sitting either on the floor on colourful rugs or on low couches covered in red velvet.

Some of them were young but a large number were old with wrinkled faces and greying hair.

These all wore a profusion of jewellery and Nevada guessed they were relatives of the Sheik, all of whom she had learnt lived in the women's quarters of a Kasbah.

Someone took her *haik* from her and when the women saw her caftan it obviously interested them and they were impressed.

Several of them wore embroidered caftans like hers and others had the beautiful addition of a *mansouriah*, an outer caftan of light veiling.

It made those who wore it seem to be cloaked in a soft-coloured mist.

A grey-haired woman beckoned to Nevada to sit beside her on the couch, and another younger woman, who was dressed so plainly that Nevada suspected that she was a slave, brought her a glass of mint tea.

It was hot and sweet, but at the same time it was more thirst-quenching than anything she had ever drunk.

As soon as she finished her glass it was filled again and now she sipped it more slowly, looking round her and knowing that to be in the Harem was as adventure few European women had experienced.

With sign-language the women admired her jewellery and showed her theirs.

Some of them had very heavy amber necklaces, others had gold and silver pieces set with huge amethysts which came from the High Atlas Mountains, turquoises, corals, and many other stones that Nevada did not recognise but which she guessed were mined somewhere in the vicinity.

There were so many things that she would have liked to know, so many things she would have liked to ask.

She wished now that instead of fighting with Tyrone Strome she had taken the opportunity when they were on the yacht to learn at least a few words of Arabic.

When she had almost exhausted her entire repertoire of mime, another woman appeared carrying a small baby in her arms.

The others pointed to Nevada and obviously explained who she was.

"*Vous parlez Français?*" the new woman said at length with a very pronounced accent which made even her French difficult to understand.

"*Oui, oui,*" Nevada replied eagerly.

It was difficult because not only was the new woman's French very limited but she spoke so badly it was hard to make sense of what she said, but somehow they managed to communicate with each other.

Nevada learnt, as she had expected, that the elderly women consisted of the mother, grandmother, sisters, and aunts of the Sheik.

He had four main wives who were allowed him by his religion, and the younger teenaged girls were concubines.

They had pale skins, little more than faintly coffee-coloured, and their features were exquisite, their faces very attractive.

Their hair was dark, long, silky, and everyone, Nevada realised, had a queenly carriage that would have made them outstanding in any country in the world.

Two were so beautiful that she thought they would have been an instantaneous success in New York or London.

They had huge dark eyes, short noses, full curved lips, and to Nevada their self-assurance was extraordinary.

They did not giggle self-consciously as schoolgirls did in New York, nor did they look shy, or stare at her rudely as she might have expected.

Their smiles were charming and friendly and by the time they all sat down to a meal, Nevada, despite the fact that she could not communicate except through the woman who spoke French, no longer felt afraid.

As they sat on cushions or on the rugs, slave girls served them a soup which was a meal in itself and was known as a *harira*. It contained chicken, dried mutton, chick peas, parsley, ginger, onions, and saffron.

When these ingredients were well cooked, they were mixed with a platter of rice seasoned with spices.

To this was added tomatoes, bread yeast and eggs.

Two bowlsful of the *harira* were, Nevada found, very filling especially as it was followed by the traditional Moorish sweetmeats made of honey and almonds which were simply delicious.

The meal was followed by the inevitable mint tea, and as soon as they had finished all the women jumped up and almost as if by magic their *lithams* appeared and they put them over their noses.

Nevada looked enquiringly at the woman who spoke French.

"Dancing," she explained. "We go see dancing."

"Where?" Nevada enquired.

But this was too difficult to explain and she merely took Nevada by the hand and pulled her along the corridor following the others.

Nevada found herself on a terrace enclosed with white lattice-work which circled all sides of a huge open court-yard.

Below she could see a number of white-robed Sheiks seated on cushions, their feet on brightly coloured carpets, and in the centre of them on the right of his host was Tyrone Strome!

He looked very proud and arrogant, Nevada thought, and at the same time very much at his ease.

The court-yard was lit by the star-strewn sky above and the light from two fires on either side, made of burning palm leaves.

Quite suddenly Nevada felt a surge of rebellious indignation at the manner in which she was being treated. How dare Tyrone Strome force her, a white woman, an American, rich and important in the Social world, to peep at him through lattice-work!

Without considering the consequences of her action, she pulled off her *litham* and ran along the terrace and down some steps she could see in one corner which led into the court-yard.

It took her only a few seconds to continue running across the empty space towards the Sheiks. She stood confronting them, the flames from the fires glittering on her red hair and her angry eyes.

"*Messieurs,*" Nevada cried loudly, and when the Sheiks' faces were all turned towards her in surprise she continued speaking in French:

"I have been brought here against my will. If any one of you will escort me to the nearest British or French Consulate, I will reward you with any sum of money you wish to ask!"

She paused. The Sheiks were all staring at her

and she thought they must understand what she was saying.

"I am rich . . . very rich," she continued. "Help me . . . please help me."

Her voice, which had rung out in the court-yard, died away and she waited.

Sheik Hassam turned his head to speak to the Moor next to him, and another bearded Sheik on Tyrone Strome's left leant backwards to whisper in his ear.

Nevada looked from one to another. Surely, she thought, someone would come to her rescue.

Then Tyrone Strome spoke to her in English.

"No-one has understood you," he said coldly. "They only speak Berber. But the gentleman beside me has offered a camel and four sheep for you. He said he likes women with spirit because it amuses him to beat it out of them."

Nevada felt her heart thump, but her eyes, with a defiant effort, met his.

"Shall I accept his offer?" he asked. "It is quite a good price for a woman in this part of the world."

"How dare you!"

For a moment Nevada forgot the Sheiks, her surroundings, in fact everything but Tyrone Strome and her persistent battle with him.

"The decision is yours!" he insisted. "It is a matter of indifference to me."

She drew in her breath. She had the terrifying feeling that he might actually hand her over to the Sheik and she would be lost.

Yet her pride made her stand staring at him, her eyes blazing with anger. Then she capitulated. With a sound that was a cry of despair, she turned and ran from the court-yard.

As she reached the steps up to the terrace she heard the Sheiks laughing.

On the terrace the women looked at her, when she joined them, with horror. Then, too polite to embarrass her, they concentrated on what was happening below.

Now there was the sound of music and Nevada realised that the women had moved their positions and were above the Sheiks.

Twenty musicians had seated themselves at the far end of the court-yard and were playing drums augmented by reed pipes and *bendirs,* a type of tambourine.

The music had a strong, rhythmic beat and a second later several dancers appeared in the centre of the court-yard.

The dancers were in muslins and silks and wore a profusion of jewellery.

"These are the Tiznet dancers," the woman who spoke French whispered to Nevada, "very famous, very exciting."

Nevada remembered that in one book of Tyrone Strome's she had read that the Tiznet dancers could rival all other dancers in North Africa including the Ouled Nails, who were notorious for their sensual and exotic movements.

The dance the Tiznet girls were doing was, she thought, similar to the Turkish "belly-dance." The girls stood almost immobile while their whole bodies shook and quivered.

The golden light from the fires made their bodies throw huge dark shadows which gave the scene a strange and almost sinister appearance.

As they danced, somewhere from the court-yard came the sound of high-pitched chanting which mingled with the music.

The dance finished and while the dancers remained in a semi-circle into the centre of them came a woman who made Nevada draw in her breath.

She was obviously very young and her figure was exquisite; her long hair was loose and covered with jewels and blue veils.

"She dances *la Guedra,*" the woman who spoke French whispered in Nevada's ear.

The dancer knelt down, her eyes closed, and her dance began with the quivering of the wrists, then it progressed to the arms, the neck, the head, the torso, the hips, and finally the whole body.

It seemed as if some internal flame swept gradually through her, growing, expanding, until at last it devoured her.

As she moved and her blue veils slipped, Nevada realised that she was naked above the waist!

Swaying, abandoning herself to the beat with every contortion of her lissom body, she was the embodiment of everything that was sensual.

Nevada could only watch, realising that the dancer was growing more and more abandoned, moving more and more quickly, her arms seeming to writhe like serpents, her eyes closed, her lips parted until it was obvious she attained a state of ecstasy.

She was fascinating, voluptuous, passionate, and she not only aroused the Sheiks but also the women who watched her.

Their breath, too, was coming quickly and they seemed almost hypnotised as their bodies were also moving and quivering in time to the rhythm and the beat.

Suddenly the end came. The dancer reached the climax of her gyrating and appeared to collapse. The drums died away into a sudden silence in which one could hear a heart-beat.

The silence seemed to hold everyone spellbound until Sheik Hassam El Zigli, with a gesture of his hands towards the Tiznet dancers who had stood in a semi-circle, drew them forward.

Each girl ran towards the Sheiks, each choosing one to throw herself down at his feet, her head bowed, her hands pressed together in the traditional attitude of abject obedience.

Then as Nevada watched, the dancer opened her eyes and Sheik Hassam, taking her hand, drew her to her feet and led her towards Tyrone Strome.

Nevada saw him look up at her, saw the smile on his lips, and with a feeling of horror and disgust she turned away!

Chapter Five

Swaying in the litter on top of the camel's back, Nevada wondered if she could sleep.

She was feeling exceedingly tired as she had been unable to rest during the night, but had tossed and turned, feeling that every sound from the other women in the room was an irritant.

Perpetually in front of her eyes she seemed to see the dancer performing her exotic gyrations as she danced the *Guedra*.

Never had Nevada imagined that any dance could be so sensuous, so provocative, and at the same time so hypnotic.

Long after she and the women had returned to their quarters she saw how emotionally they had been aroused and affected by the music and the passionate climax of the *Guedra*.

Besides this, the youngest wife of the Sheik was in tears, and the woman who spoke French explained that it was because she was jealous.

"She loves our master," she whispered to Nevada, "and after the dancers come he will not send for her for perhaps two or three days."

It seemed strange, Nevada thought, that the Sheik's fourth wife, who was very attractive and could not have been more than eighteen years of age, should love him so much.

Then she remembered that as he was in fact the only man the women ever knew they had no other choice.

It was impossible, once they were all settled down for the night, for Nevada not to think of Tyrone Strome and the way he had smiled at the dancer.

It seemed almost as if his face was sketched on the darkness and she could see only too clearly the movement of his lips and what she thought was a glimmer of fire in his eyes.

The Sheik's mother had made Nevada as comfortable as possible, giving her a place of honour on the *matelas*, a low sofa which consisted of velvet-covered mattresses resting on long wooden supports.

It was in fact very comfortable, but sleep eluded her and when the morning came she felt hollow-eyed and exhausted in a way she had never known before.

They were aroused early, being informed by a slave that Tyrone Strome wished to leave soon after dawn.

Nevada was touched by the manner in which the Sheik's mother and the other women bade her farewell almost affectionately.

Their good wishes for the journey and the hope that she would visit them again were all conveyed to her by the woman who spoke French.

Then with many salaams and hands pressed together touching first the forehead, then the lips and the breast, Nevada followed a servant down the twisting passages to the room where the Sheik had received them on arrival.

When she arrived there, she was ignored, as indeed she had expected, both by the Sheik and by Tyrone Strome.

Only by a glance in her direction did he direct her to follow him when he went outside the house to where a horse and a camel were waiting for them.

The rest of the caravan joined them at the outer gate of the Kasbah and they left amongst a noisy farewell from the Sheik's servants and the cries of children who ran excitedly beside them for a little distance in the desert itself.

There was a cold wind blowing as they set off, which soon died away as the sun rose, and every hour they travelled the heat grew in intensity.

Soon they were in very different country from that which Nevada had seen before.

Huge rocks rose on either side of narrow, stony valleys through which their path wound and climbed; there were dry gorges and crumbling granite hill-sides, pock-marked with caves.

Once they crossed a shallow Souss river with the water pitiably scarce between rocky boulders. Soon there were hot and bare infertile hills where only argan trees grew.

The continuous motion caused Nevada's eye-lids to droop and she was in fact half-asleep when unexpectedly the caravan came to a halt.

She opened her eyes to see that they were in a rocky defile with great granite cliffs rising on either side of them.

Then she saw Tyrone Strome, who obviously had been riding far ahead of the rest of them, come hurrying back on his horse, passing the camels and the donkeys until he reached her side.

He gave a sharp order to her camel-driver, who in his turn ordered the camel to kneel.

Slowly, grunting as it did so, the animal obeyed and now Tyrone Strome said to Nevada:

"Get down, and hurry!"

She looked at him in surprise. Then she thought that perhaps again he had something unpleasant to show her as he had the day before, when he had taken her to see the corpse of the man who had been murdered.

She wanted to argue, to protest, but now he was giving fluent commands to the camel-driver and even as she moved, the man started to take the litter from the top of the camel's back.

Standing on the rough stony path, Nevada

watched him in astonishment. Then she felt Tyrone Strome take her wrist.

He had dismounted and his horse was being led away.

"What is happening?" she asked.

"Come with me! I will explain later."

He pulled her forward as he spoke, dragging her over the stones at a speed which again hurt her feet in their thin *babouches*.

She tripped and gave a little cry.

He loosened his hold on her wrist and impatiently without an explanation picked her up in his arms.

She was too astonished to say anything as he climbed up the side of the cliff until having reached some large boulders he set her down behind them and knelt down to peer back into the valley at the caravan below them.

She followed the direction of his eyes and saw that the litter had now not only been removed from the camel on which she had been riding but had been smashed by the driver and the pieces thrown over some rocks where they were out of sight.

As the man finished doing this he ordered the camel to its feet and the caravan began slowly to move forward again, Tyrone Strome's horse, now with a large bundle on its back, being led by a boy.

"What is happening? Why are they leaving us?" Nevada asked nervously.

She could not understand what was occurring or why Tyrone Strome was behaving in such a strange manner.

For a moment she thought he was not going to reply. Then he answered in a low voice:

"There are horsemen approaching us."

"Horsemen?" she questioned. "Who are they?"

"I do not know for certain, but I am taking no chances!"

"But why? Do you think they might attack us?"

"They may be the servants of the Sheik who offered for you last night," he said harshly. "A white woman is an attraction in this part of the world, and later in the evening he increased the amount he was prepared to pay for you."

There was something contemptuous in his voice that made Nevada feel ashamed.

"I am . . . sorry," she murmured.

"On the other hand, they may just be thieves intent on robbing a caravan," he continued. "There are quite a large number of marauding bands of that sort and we might be unfortunate enough to encounter one."

As he spoke he drew a revolver from beneath his white robes.

"You mean . . . to fight them?"

"If I have to. It will mean bloodshed and death, but doubtless you will find that interesting."

Nevada looked down at the colourful caravan beneath them moving through the pass between brown rocks.

"Please . . . do not say that . . . again," she pleaded in a low voice. "You have punished me enough for what I said to David without . . . thinking. I shall never forget the . . . skeleton we saw yesterday."

There was a note in her voice which told Tyrone Strome she spoke in all sincerity, and because they were close to each other he was aware of the little shudder that went through her as she remembered the empty eye-sockets in the skull and the bared teeth.

There was no time to reply, for at that moment at the far end of the defile there appeared a number of horsemen wearing the traditional floating white robes, each of them bearing in their hands a long-barrelled black gun.

They drew in their horses in front of the caravan, pulling them sharply back on their haunches in the manner that Arab riders had perfected in their wild charge known as the *fantasia.*

Then the leader began to talk to the man leading the caravan.

Tyrone Strome listened intently to what was being said, and Nevada, watching his grim expression, felt suddenly more afraid than she had ever been in her whole life.

Almost instinctively she moved nearer to him and as she did so he realised that she was trembling convulsively.

He was holding his revolver in his right hand. Now he put his left arm round Nevada, and although she was not certain whether it was an action of protection or merely to prevent her from making any movement which might attract attention, it was curiously comforting.

It was no use trying to be an independent woman in a situation like this, she told herself. She wished she could cling even closer to Tyrone Strome and hide her face against him so that she would not see what happened when the shooting started.

Her heart was beating frantically in her breast and she expected every moment to see the men in the valley beneath them shot down by the horsemen and Tyrone Strome forced to join in.

But as she held her breath the conversation in which now several of the other horsemen had joined came to an end.

Having given a shout which seemed to combine an order and at the same time a cry of elation, they were moving at what seemed a dangerous speed down the defile in the direction of the Kasbah.

Because she was close against him Nevada felt the sigh of relief Tyrone Strome gave which made no sound between his lips but which released the tension of his body.

"They have . . . gone," she said in a voice that was hardly above a whisper.

"To look for you," he answered. "I was right, the Sheik who saw you last night without your *litham* is determined to include you in his Harem!"

Nevada drew in her breath, then she said:

"I am sorry . . . forgive me . . . I realise now it was a . . . foolish thing to do."

"It was not only foolish but also exceedingly dangerous," Tyrone Strome answered. "Come, we must get out of this."

He pulled her to her feet, hurried ahead of her down the side of the cliff to where the caravan was waiting, and spoke to the men.

Then as the bundle was taken from his horse's saddle and a boy brought it to their side he said to Nevada:

"As it will be easy for the Sheik's horsemen to discover you are not, as they now think, at the Kasbah, you and I must take the risk of travelling alone without an escort."

As Nevada looked at him questioningly he picked her up in his arms and lifted her onto the saddle of his horse.

She sat sideways as an Eastern woman would and he sprang up behind her, encircling her once again with his left arm while he took the reins in his right hand.

He gave some further orders to the leader of the caravan and Nevada thought that he told them to make all possible speed towards where they were going.

Then he spurred the horse into action and it moved sure-footedly over the rough stones and out of the defile onto the uneven stony ground that lay ahead of them.

They rode for some way before Nevada said:

"Have we far to go?"

"Far enough," Tyrone Strome replied.

"You mean that the horsemen may . . . overtake us when they find I am . . . not at the Kasbah?"

"It is a possibility."

"And if they . . . do?"

There was silence for a moment, then Tyrone Strome said:

"You will have the choice of either going with them or dying at my hand."

Because she could not help herself Nevada turned and hid her face against his shoulder.

"There is no . . . question of there being any . . . choice," she said when she could control her voice. "You know I would rather . . . die."

"That is what I expected you to say," he answered. "But if we are lucky and the gods are propitious, we shall reach Tafraout and safety before they can return."

Her face was still hidden against his shoulder and after a moment she whispered:

"I am sorry . . . I am really . . . I did not . . . understand that a Sheik might feel like that about me . . . I only wanted . . . help."

"And you really imagined that was what they would give you?" Tyrone Strome asked, and now there was a note of amusement in his voice.

"I read in your books that they were . . . uncivilised, but I suppose because I am so . . . ignorant it meant nothing."

"It is not so much a question of their being uncivilised," he answered, "but the fact is that women have little value in their eyes except as creatures of amusement. That women may have feelings or preferences as to who becomes their master is a consideration which never arises."

Nevada did not reply.

She was thinking that perhaps that was what he himself felt about women.

He had certainly never considered her feelings, and yet at the moment he was risking his life and the lives of a number of other men to save her from the consequences of her own stupidity.

She was well aware that if it came to a fight the camel-drivers could easily be gunned down by the armed horsemen, and Tyrone Strome's revolver was not likely to prove very effective for long.

She wondered what he would feel if he was forced to kill her as he had offered to do.

Then she told herself that he must have killed many people in his life and one woman more would not be of much consequence one way or the other.

Because her conflicting thoughts were mingled with fear, they were more upsetting than anything she had ever experienced in her life.

She could only shut her eyes and lie limply in his arms as they moved more swiftly than it seemed possible over the uneven, rocky ground.

'I am safe for the moment,' Nevada thought, 'safe because he is holding me and because he will protect me . . . while he can.'

She tried to reckon how many miles they had progressed since leaving the Kasbah and it seemed to her it could not be very many because the caravan moved so slowly.

The horsemen on their fiery Arab steeds would reach it in a quarter of the time, then they would return.

She felt her heart beating tumultuously at the fear such thoughts engendered, and yet even though she was frightened she could not really visualise what she feared becoming reality.

Could it be possible that she, Nevada Van Arden, a pampered rich American, could die in this stony desert and no-one would even know it had occurred?

When she thought of it she realised with a sense of horror how little her death would matter.

How many real friends had she who would mourn the fact that she was no longer with them? How many people loved her enough to weep one tear when they heard that she was dead?

For the first time Nevada saw herself as she was, without the frame of her wealth, without even the importance of her beauty.

If she died as the man Tyrone Strome had shown her yesterday had died, the vultures would pick the flesh from her bones and she would only be another skeleton lying bleached in the sunshine.

What she was feeling and indeed suffering must have communicated itself in some way to Tyrone Strome, for his arm tightened round her and he said in a kinder voice than he had used to her before:

"It is a good principle when one is in danger never to anticipate the worst."

"It is . . . difficult . . . not to," she said in a smothered voice.

"I know," he replied, "but my luck has never failed me in the past and I cannot believe it will desert me now."

"I . . . hope not," she whispered, "I do not wish . . . to die."

"Nor do I, as it happens," Tyrone Strome answered, "because I still have quite a lot to do."

"Your book to finish . . . for one thing."

"Exactly!"

She felt he was smiling above her head as he added:

"Do not forget that if we survive, this will be an adventure which will read extremely well in our memoirs."

"That of course depends on how many more adventures you have."

Because he spoke in such a matter-of-fact tone she felt the fear that had possessed her receding a little, and she managed to say in quite an ordinary voice:

"I think after this I shall be content to sit at home with my knitting."

"You might find it preferable to learn to cook."

For a moment she thought he was insulting her, then she realised that he was teasing.

"I shall certainly take lessons . . . if we ever get back to . . . civilisation."

"At the moment I cannot offer you anything very civilised," he replied, "but we are in fact in sight of safety."

There was a note of triumph in his voice which made her raise her head, and as she did so she saw perhaps a mile away an enormous pink granite cliff silhouetted against the sky and at its foot the feathery green of palm trees.

"Tafraout!" she exclaimed excitedly.

She looked at him as she spoke and saw the smile on his lips.

'Once again he was won!' she thought.

Now it seemed that her terror and her fears had been senseless because she should have known it was inevitable that in anything he undertook Tyrone Strome would always be successful.

They drew nearer and she saw that besides palms there were olive and almond trees encircling a small town whose walls and houses were all pink.

There were many small Kasbahs which she recognised by their crenellated towers, and as they drew nearer still Nevada discovered that Tafraout lay at the top of a valley which was surprisingly fertile and also exceedingly beautiful.

Right in the heart of a gigantic mountain range, isolated from the rest of Morocco, Tafraout was a tiny Shangri-la hidden from a hostile world.

Its high granite cliffs enclosed it like protective arms, in places their sheer walls rising hundreds of feet and making the whole place a natural fortress.

It had an enchantment that made Nevada wonder as they reached the valley if perhaps she was dreaming.

As if he knew what she was thinking Tyrone Strome said:

"The Ammeln Valley is the equivalent of some of the strange, fantastically fertile valleys I have seen amongst the mountains of the Himalayas. Here you will find a secret, age-old civilisation which is different from anything elsewhere in Morocco."

"Tell me about it," Nevada asked eagerly.

"Later," he answered. "I think we should first reach my house."

"Your . . . house?"

He nodded and now the horse was moving slowly through narrow streets until they came to a pink Kasbah surrounded by almond trees which gave it the ethereal beauty of a fairy-tale Palace.

The heavy doors were opened, and when they appeared, servants came hurrying out to welcome

Tyrone Strome with smiling faces and endless salaams.

He spoke to them in their own language and led the way inside.

It was in fact more a house than a Kasbah, and when they dismounted at yet another door Tyrone Strome lifted Nevada to the ground.

She entered the house to find one of the most exquisite Moorish rooms she had ever seen.

The tiles, the hangings, and the lattice-work were all far more beautiful than she had ever imagined and there seemed to be exceptional comfort in Western style in the large couches covered with silk cushions and the cool fans working in the ceiling above them.

Tyrone Strome invited Nevada with a gesture to sit down on one of the couches and as soon as she did so a cup of mint tea was set before her.

She looked up at him questioningly and he said with a smile:

"You may take off your *haik* and your *litham* here and be comfortable."

Eagerly Nevada threw back her white covering and pulled the *litham* from her nose.

Her hair was unbound and it fell over her shoulders vividly red in the soft light which came from hidden windows.

She thought she must look shockingly untidy after all she had been through, but for the moment she did not care.

She picked up the cup of mint tea and drank it thankfully, realising as she did so that she was desperately thirsty not only from the long ride but also from the fear she had endured.

Tyrone Strome went from the room and she looked about her.

It seemed extraordinary that this should be his house, and yet from the quick glance she had had at the valley she could understand anyone who liked solitude and strange places wishing to come to Tafraout.

'He is able to work here,' she thought, and because she knew he must be anxious about the caravan, when he came back she asked:

"Is there any sign of it?"

"I have sent several of my men out to escort it in," he answered.

"You are worried about the manuscript of your book."

"How did you know?" he enquired.

"How much have you done already?"

"Nearly half. I should find it extremely boring to have to begin again from the beginning."

"Then we can only pray that it arrives safely."

He raised his eye-brows before he said:

"That is hardly the sentiment of an enemy. You should be hoping that I would be distraught by the loss of such a valuable piece of property."

"I am not quite as petty as that," Nevada replied quickly, then realised that he was teasing her.

"Where do you work?" she asked.

He indicated a table she had not noticed before, at the far end of the room.

He went towards it and pulled back some exquisitely embroidered hangings to reveal a large glassless window which overlooked the whole valley.

Nevada rose to her feet to join him and stand staring at the cultivation, the blossoms on the trees, the flowers, the pink buildings, and the huge rose-tinted cliffs glinting with a strange reflected light.

Between boulders like giant rocks there snuggled occasionally little villages, the colours of their houses so like the landscape that they were almost invisible.

"The Ammeln Valley!" Tyrone Strome said.

"It is very beautiful."

"That is what I felt when I first came here, and found it surprising and mysterious."

"Almost as if you dreamt it," she added.

He did not answer and after a moment she asked:

"You are writing about it in your book?"

"Yes."

"Could I help you?"

"To write my book?" he questioned.

"No, of course not," she replied, "but perhaps I could copy out what you are writing. I have always heard that authors make many different copies before their manuscript is finally published."

"It is certainly an idea," he answered, "but I suspect you would find it boring."

"I would be far more bored if I had nothing to do," Nevada said, "although at the moment I feel I could sit for twenty-four hours a day just looking out this window at the valley."

"Even though the view may feed the spirit," Tyrone Strome smiled, "I suspect that you are feeling hungry, as I am. Let me show you to your room. I have told my servants to leave you a change of clothing; I only hope one of the caftans they bring you will fit, but tomorrow you will be able to purchase more to your own taste."

Nevada was surprised, but she said nothing. She merely followed him to where on the same floor there was a luxurious bed-room also with a window which looked out over the valley.

Again, as was usual in Morocco, there was no glass in it, but there were huge wooden shutters which could be closed when it was cold.

It was such a large and comfortable room that Nevada said:

"I am sure this is really your room. I would not wish as an unwanted guest to deprive you of it."

Tyrone Strome smiled, at the same time she had a feeling that her considerateness surprised him.

"I assure you," he replied, "that this is where I entertain my visitors. My own room is next door, and while you are here in the safety of my Kasbah I promise you will not be kidnapped or robbed. You will not be aware of it but you will in fact be very effectively guarded."

Nevada looked at him nervously.

"You think the Sheik's men might still come in search of me?"

"There is always a possibility that the Sheik himself will not give up the chase," Tyrone Strome replied. "But the citizens of Tafraout are a law unto themselves; they do not form a tribe but are a distinct people and their country's borders are marked by the mountains."

"You say the Tafraoutis are not a tribe," Nevada said. "Then what are they?"

Tyrone Strome laughed.

"That is a question that has been asked for centuries by the Moroccans themselves. The Tafraoutis are in fact the oldest, truest, and most untouched people in the nation."

He saw the interest in Nevada's eyes and went on:

"They are Berbers of the Chileun group who fled to these mountains twelve hundred years ago to escape the encroachment of the Arab conquerors. They can be very aggressive to the outside world and they are very possessive about their own valley. They work hard and 'keep themselves very much to themselves,' as the English say."

Tyrone Strome walked to the window and looked at the valley as he went on:

"If a Tafraouti man leaves here to make his fortune in some other part of Morocco, he invariably comes home to marry. He builds one of those flat-roofed fortress-like houses in rose colour, and when he retires he will sire a family and live, happily ever after, in this little Eden."

His voice sounded almost envious, Nevada thought, and after a moment she asked:

"Is that what you want to do?"

"Perhaps, one day when I am too old to go adventuring," he answered lightly.

He walked towards the door.

"I have arranged for a maid to look after you, but I am afraid you will have to communicate with her in sign-language."

The maid proved to be an attractive young girl. She was shy but anxious to please and she carried in warm water and produced, as Tyrone Strome had promised, several caftans into which Nevada could change.

Most of them were too small, but there was one of a lovely shade of pale green embroidered in gold which fitted her.

There were new slippers for her feet, and because she felt it was silly not to wear it she put on the gold jewellery which Tyrone Strome had given her for the journey.

There was a mirror in her room in which she could see herself reflected and she thought as she looked at her long red hair hanging over her shoulders that it would be hard to find even in the most expensive Paris shops anything that became her better.

The long straight caftan was made of soft silk and it clung to the outlines of her body and revealed rather than concealed her slim shape.

Nevada could not help realising what a tremendous impression her present appearance would make on any of the men in New York, Paris, and London who had paid her such extravagant compliments and laid their hearts at her feet.

'What a pity there is no-one here to admire me,' she thought.

She was well aware of Tyrone Strome's feelings where she was concerned.

He had made it very clear how much he despised her and had called her a vixen. Angry though it made her, she now realised that there was in fact some justification for his insult.

Once again she could see the skull of the dead man lying in the bright sunshine and hear her own voice telling David mockingly that it would be interesting to see a dead man.

And if Tyrone Strome had not acted so quickly, if he had not seen the Sheik's men before they reached the caravan, there might have been a dozen men dead or dying lying amongst the rocks and she herself dead from the last bullet in his revolver.

Nevada turned away from the mirror as if she could not bear to look at her own reflection.

"How could I have known," she asked, "that in other parts of the world men live by the gun and what is important is to stay alive?"

She had never realised before, she thought, how precious life was, or how difficult it could be to preserve it.

Now it seemed to her she had cheapened something that was beyond price, beyond value—life itself—the mere act of breathing and of being.

She knew very little about Tyrone Strome, but she had heard David talk about him with the reverence which a young man gives to someone who is a hero in his own field.

Vaguely she knew that he had done many dangerous and gallant things in his life, which nevertheless were so secret that he would not talk about them.

No wonder, she thought, if he had been in many situations such as they had experienced today, that he should think it sordid and revolting that a woman should laugh at death or think it amusing to see a dead body.

"I am not really like that," Nevada whispered to herself. "Or . . . am I?"

As she went back to the Sitting-Room to find Tyrone Strome she somehow felt shy.

It had been one thing to sit with him wearing native dress in an oasis, but to eat alone in his house with her hair falling loose over her shoulders and wearing nothing beneath a silk caftan made her unaccountably self-conscious.

There was a meal waiting for them which was to be served at a low table, Eastern fashion, in front of the comfortable couch piled with silk cushions.

But if Nevada was shy, Tyrone Strome was very much at his ease.

"I feel you are in need of a glass of wine," he said, "which is something which will never be offered you in a Moslem house. However, here we are beyond any religious restrictions, so I hope you will enjoy it."

The wine was in fact delicious and made Nevada think of the sunshine outside.

Because it was after midday and the heat was intense Tyrone Strome had drawn the curtains again over the window and the room was dim and cool.

The food, which was Moorish, was delicious, and because Nevada was hungry she ate without speaking until as the sweetmeats were put on the table she leaned back with a sigh to say:

"If I have seemed greedy you must forgive me."

"I was hungry too," he said. "I think relief from fear is always a good appetizer."

"I was . . . very frightened."

"I realised that."

She felt he was remembering how she had trembled when the horsemen had entered the valley, and she felt ashamed that she had not been more brave.

"I think perhaps you now realise that in situations such as we have encountered today," Tyrone Strome said, "a woman, however independent she may feel herself, needs the protection of a man."

"You know I know that now," Nevada replied. "There is no need to make me feel more humble than I am already."

"Humble? Are you really humble, Nevada?" he asked. "It is the last thing I would have expected you to be."

"I know only too well what you think of me," Nevada answered, "and I suppose my only excuse can be that I was completely ignorant. It is very easy to be brave when you do not know what you are talking about; and perhaps it is easy too not to understand people's feelings if you have never felt them yourself."

"That is a generous admission," Tyrone Strome said quietly.

Nevada rose from the couch to walk towards the window. She pulled back one of the curtains to look out. The sunshine on the valley was almost blinding.

The colours of the pink cliffs dazzled her eyes.

"How long are we going to stay here?" she asked.

"That rather depends," Tyrone Strome replied. "Are you in such a hurry to leave?"

"Not now," she answered.

"Why not?"

"Because I am curious—curious about the people, about this place, and . . ."

She did not finish the sentence and after a moment Tyrone Strome asked:

"What else?"

"If you want the truth . . . about you."

"In what way?"

"I would like to know why you took it upon yourself, so far as I was concerned, to play God. Oh, I know it was to save David. But you could have disposed of me quite effectively without bringing me here to a secret place which I feel is very important to you."

She spoke quietly and when she ceased speaking it seemed as if the silence between them had something unusual about it.

As he did not answer, Nevada drew the curtain closed again and turned back into the room.

For a moment because her eyes were blinded by the sun she could not see anything, then gradually she realised he was still lying back on the couch and his eyes as she moved towards him were on her face.

She walked slowly until she stood in front of him, her eyes very green in her pale face, and there was a question in them, as if the answer she waited for was of importance.

Tyrone Strome did not speak for some seconds.

His eyes held Nevada's and she felt as if he looked deep into her, searchingly, seekingly. Then very quietly but with a twist to his lips which somehow robbed the words of any pomposity he said:

"I think, Nevada, you have begun to learn a little about yourself."

Chapter Six

Looking out the window of her bed-room, Nevada was once again lost in the beauty of the scene outside.

Directly below her there was a sharp drop to the wall surrounding the Kasbah, which was brilliant with flowering trees.

Beyond, farther down the hill, was the winding path which led to the small town of Tafraout, and her eyes looked beyond again to where the valley lay brilliant in the sunshine with the mountains on each side of it reflecting every shade of pink.

Whenever she looked at the Ammeln Valley it seemed to be more lovely than it had been before.

It was hard to remember that only a short distance away there were the bare infertile valleys, granite cliffs, and stony ground through which they had travelled to get here.

It was now a week since she had come to Tyrone Strome's Kasbah, and yet the time had passed very quickly.

Sometimes she felt that she had known no other type of existence but had always lived in this peace and quiet, surrounded by a beauty that spoke not only to the mind but also to the soul.

In front of her on an improvised desk there was Tyrone Strome's manuscript, which she was copying neatly onto a stack of plain paper.

She had expected, because he had said he was writing a history, that it would be rather heavy and perhaps as hard to read as some of the books he had lent her while she was on the yacht.

But she thought now that she might have expected anything he wrote to be as individualistic and original as he was himself.

He made the tribes of whom he wrote come to life, he made them human beings with problems and difficulties, who laughed and cried, strove to better themselves, and faced defeat with courage.

Every page she copied from his original manuscript made Nevada not only more interested in the Berbers, but also more intrigued and insatiably curious about the writer.

To her Tyrone Strome had always been stern and contemptuous; but she found he had a great sense of the ridiculous, besides a compassion and understanding which made some things he wrote bring her near to tears.

She realised both in reading what he had written and in her conversations with him that he was not only a very talented man but also in some ways a very enigmatic one.

Every hour, she thought, she learnt new things about him and discovered different facets of his character that she had not known before.

"I am sure there is no-one in the world like him," she murmured now, looking out onto the valley.

Then almost as if her thoughts conjured him up she saw him coming up the path from the village.

He was riding his horse and walking beside him were several turbaned men in *djellabas*, talking animatedly and gesticulating with their hands. He was giving them, Nevada knew, his undivided attention.

She had learnt now and appreciated his one-pointed concentration on anyone in whom he was interested.

It might be a man—and there were many of them who called to discuss their personal troubles and difficulties—or a child whom he had found crying in the street and whom he would stop to comfort.

Nothing was too small or too insignificant to command his attention. Nevada would watch him and reason that he was so exceptional because he seldom seemed to be thinking about himself.

She lived a strange life in the pink Kasbah, which was like no other existence she had ever known or imagined.

They breakfasted together every day as soon as Tyrone Strome returned from riding.

He usually left the Kasbah long before she was awake, and although she would have liked to accompany him she was too shy to suggest it.

When he returned the sun was rising, and yet it was still cool and they would eat in the court-yard round which the Kasbah was built.

There were exotic plants, flowers, and even fruit trees in the convenient space, and a small stone fountain whose rising and falling water made a musical accompaniment to anything they said.

As soon as breakfast was over Tyrone Strome would start work and because there was nothing else for her to do Nevada would work too.

She had the idea that he wanted her to be alone, as she had been on the yacht, with no-one to talk to and nothing to occupy her.

But after she had suggested she could fair-copy his manuscript, he had taken her at her word and had set in front of her what pages of his book were completed.

She had begun immediately to copy them out, frequently finding it difficult to follow his alterations, his inserts, and to be correct in the spelling of some of the native words he used.

They would not meet again until luncheon, and after a light but delicious meal was finished the whole Kasbah became very quiet; for it was the time of the siesta and everyone slept.

It was then that Tyrone Strome would talk to

Nevada in the cool Sitting-Room with the curtains drawn and the fans waving over their heads to keep the air moving.

At first she had been nervous of asking him questions in case he snubbed her, but as they sat or lay comfortably in the deep couches she was brave enough now to ask many things she wished to know.

Not about his career. She was quite certain he would not tell her about that.

Yet she had learnt that no other Englishman could have moved about South Morocco as he did or built a house in Tafraout.

"The tribes are fiercely suspicious of foreigners and infidels," he told Nevada, "and travellers are received with a suspicion which usually ends in death."

"But you are different?"

"They have grown to trust me for various reasons," he replied evasively. "When I first came here I was handed from one tribe to another, always carrying a special spear talisman until I reached the borders of another tribal territory."

He laughed and added:

"Where we are now is so secret it is marked on the map as: 'the Saharan Mountains, relatively unpopulated.'"

If Tyrone Strome would tell Nevada no more about his work, he did tell her about the places he had seen, the people he had met, and in the last two days about his thoughts and philosophy.

'I have learnt more here than I have ever learnt before in all the years of my life,' Nevada thought now, her eyes on Tyrone Strome as he rode up the path.

With the sun behind him he seemed to be coming towards her haloed in light, and she thought no other man could be as aggressively male or have such a compelling personality. But because she wanted to hear what he had to tell her she tried not to provoke him.

"There is so much he can teach me," she told

herself. "I would be foolish not to take what advantage I can by being in his company . . . willingly or unwillingly."

Suddenly she remembered that one day—it might be tomorrow, it might be weeks ahead—he would decide to leave.

He would take her back—back to the Social world with which she was so familiar. That was what she had longed for. But quite unexpectedly, with the violent impact of a pistol-shot, she realised she had no wish to go.

There was no need to ask herself why.

It was as if the ground had opened, there was a deep pit at her feet, and the voices of demons jeered at her because she wanted to stay with him.

She gave a cry which came from the depths of her being.

"No! No!" she whispered. "I hate him . . . hate and loathe him . . . for the way he has treated me!"

She could hear the fiendish laughter her words evoked:

"You love him—you love him!"

"No, I hate him!"

But while her mind insisted she hated Tyrone Strome, her heart told her the truth—she loved him!

"Oh, God, it cannot be true . . . it is impossible!" she said frantically.

Yet, the more she protested, the more she knew it was the truth—she loved him.

She had in fact lost her hatred when she had trembled with fear behind the boulders and known he would protect her from the Sheik's horsemen.

And when he had held her in his arms as they rode ahead of the caravan towards Tafraout it had been not only a comfort, a relief, but something more to be close to him, to hide her face against his shoulder.

But still she had not admitted it to herself, not even when she had slept that night as unafraid as a child because he was in the next room.

'I loved him then,' Nevada thought, 'but every

day it has increased until it was only my pride which would not let me acknowledge it.'

She now admitted despairingly that every morning had seemed exciting because she had known that she would see him.

The days passed quickly because she was reading his book, counting the hours until they could have luncheon together, talk afterwards, and the evenings had been an enchantment that was irresistible.

The second night when she walked into the court-yard to find him waiting for her, the table lit by candles, she had looked at the light reflected iridescently in the fountain and said mockingly:

"This is very theatrical . . . a stage-set!"

"But very romantic!"

"I would not know. You are aware I am not interested in romance."

"How much you miss!"

"I do not agree—I save myself from heart-aches and unrequited yearnings which make the people who feel them sloppy and ridiculous."

"Love has inspired men since the beginning of time to do magnificent deeds of courage, to paint and compose great masterpieces, to build a tomb as exquisite as the Taj Mahal."

"I am sorry for the women who had to endure their maudlin talk of love."

"The ways of Allah are inscrutable," Tyrone Strome replied. "He gave you the body and face of a woman and forgot to include a heart."

"For which I say a prayer of thankfulness every day of my life," Nevada retorted. "While other women writhe in chains of their own making, I am free."

She saw the amusement in Tyrone Strome's eyes and added coldly:

"I am speaking of emotional freedom! I am well aware that physically I am your prisoner."

"If I behaved as my counterpart would have done a hundred years ago, I would incarcerate you in a deep, dark dungeon. They lie beneath every Kasbah in South Morocco."

He smiled as he continued:

"The prisoners were chained together with heavy iron collars and leg shackles. They received just enough food to sustain life."

"It was barbaric!"

"I agree. They lay in darkness, sometimes shackled to a corpse, until a merciful death released them."

"So that is what would have happened to me!"

"On second thought I doubt it—your captor would undoubtedly have found a place for you in his Harem."

Thinking of how that might have been her fate, Nevada shivered. The Harem or a dungeon! How many unknown women had been given no alternative?

Last night, however, she had been unable to scoff at the insidious atmosphere of the court-yard, and she knew it bewitched her.

In a caftan of deep blue embroidered with silver stars, she felt as if she were a part of the sky above.

In a strange mood which was almost one of coquetry, she had put a blue veil over her red hair and ornamented it with brooches fashioned like stars.

Little silver bells on her anklets tinkled softly, and as she moved towards Tyrone Strome she knew, as a woman knows instinctively, that she was looking mysterious and alluring.

He looked at her with that strange expression in his eyes which she could not translate, but she felt he was acutely aware of her, as she was of him.

They talked of ordinary things, his book and some new discoveries he had made about another Moroccan tribe, but there were silences when the beauty of the flowers and the rise and fall of the fountain seemed to be speaking for them.

She had known then, she thought, although she would not acknowledge it, that she vibrated to him like an instrument in the hand of a musician.

It was as if every word he spoke had a special meaning which was assimilated not only by her mind but by her body.

He was very quiet, yet she felt as if he over-powered and dominated her until she had no life of her own and her very breathing was a part of his.

When it was time to say good-night she had risen to stand beside the fountain, feeling that the cool water soothed her as if she were feverish.

She thought he was watching her but she was not sure.

Was he aware, she wondered, that he was the cause of her restlessness, of a sudden sense of inse-curity, of tumultuous feelings raging within her breasts to which she dared not put a name?

"Good-night."

The word came to her lips because she wanted to stay, but was too afraid to do so.

"Good-night, Nevada."

There was nothing in the calm, slow words to make her heart thump and her breath come quickly.

Supposing, she thought wildly, she asked him to touch her, to kiss her good-night, as any man in the same circumstances would have tried to do?

Then she was appalled at her own thoughts. How could she think such things about any man, least of all Tyrone Strome?

She hated him. He was everything she repu-diated and which revolted her!

"Good-night!" she said again sharply, and walked from the court-yard without looking back.

Only in her bed-room behind a closed door had she lifted her hands to her burning cheeks and asked herself if the Moroccan sun had sent her mad.

❊   ❊   ❊

The morning after their arrival, as Tyrone Strome had promised, the traders from the town had brought a large selection of caftans from which Nevada could choose.

They were all beautiful, in the clear, vivid colours which the Berber women loved. The embroidery was exquisite, while some combined gold or silver thread with real turquoises, corals, and amethysts from the High Atlas Mountains.

There were also shawls, veils, and scarves that were each more attractive than the last.

Nevada had selected what she wanted and Tyrone Strome had done her bargaining for her. Not to bargain was to spoil the pleasure of the vendor, who expected every sale to be a battle of wits.

The jewellers came too, sitting cross-legged as they spread out their wares on small pieces of black velvet.

Nevada found it impossible to resist the exquisite work which craftsmen had put into silver earrings curved like crescents with fringes of precious stones or pearls.

The bangles with strange designs engraved on them were a delight, as were the anklets that went with them.

Because those which had tiny bells attached to them amused her, she wore them every evening when she walked bare-footed with hennaed feet to dine alone with Tyrone Strome in the court-yard under the stars.

"You must keep an account of everything you spend on me," she told him, "and I will pay you back. I had a lot of money with me on the yacht."

"It will be quite safe."

"We shall need a caravan of at least twenty camels to carry all my purchases," she laughed.

"It shall be arranged," he promised, "as soon as we decide to leave."

"When *you* decide," she corrected.

He smiled.

"As you say—when *I* decide to take you back."

She longed to ask him when that would be. But even as the words came to her lips she knew that to ask the question was a pretence that she was eager to go.

"I love him!" she told herself now, her eyes on him as he drew nearer the Kasbah. "However could it happen? . . . What can I do?"

Since they had come to Tafraout he had been
courteous, and considerate of her comfort in the same
way he would have treated any other woman who
was staying in his house.

But underneath the superficial courtesy there was
nothing to make her think that he had changed his
previous opinion of her.

She could hear his voice all too clearly, saying:
"You are not ordinary, Nevada, you are cruel, hard-
hearted, and, I am almost inclined to think—evil!"

His voice had been almost like a whip-lash and
she could also hear him say, his expression very grim
and stern:

"I brought you on this voyage not only to save my
nephew and young Dundonald, but also to find out
if it would be possible to turn a vixen into a woman."

"A vixen into a woman!"

The words haunted her and sometimes she would
wake in the night thinking she could hear him saying
them again, condemning her from the end of her
bed.

It had been easy then to tell herself that it was
not of the least importance to her what he thought or
felt. Once she was free of him, she would get her revenge.

She was not sure what form it would take, but
somehow she would humiliate him and make him
suffer as she was suffering.

"I hate him . . . I hate him . . . I hate him!" The
words were a talisman she recited to herself over
and over again.

"Yet now I love him!" Nevada said despairingly.
"How could I love any man who feels about me as he
does?"

Yet there was no doubt that she was in love.

She had only to see Tyrone Strome come into the
room to feel her heart turn over in her breast.

She had only to hear his voice to feel a strange
excitement rising in her throat, and when he smiled
at her it was as if the sun shone and her whole being
came to life.

Below her he had reached the wall of the Kasbah and as he turned his horse towards the entrance, they were out of sight.

Now there was only the silence and beauty of the valley, and Nevada sat looking at it, feeling that she could not miss one second of its loveliness before it was taken from her.

Once he took her back, once she became not a vixen whom he was trying to turn into a woman but herself—a rich American called Nevada Van Arden —she would be left with nothing but memories.

How long would it be before this happened?

She looked down at his manuscript and realised that he had done a great deal of work in the last week.

Perhaps the book would soon be finished.

She had no idea how long he intended it to be.

Would he then become restless? Would he want another of the adventures that meant so much to him?

Despairingly she knew the answer. He was a man who would never be content to do nothing for long.

A rest, a holiday, was one thing, but to fulfil himself he must be active.

"Suppose I never see him again?"

The question, Nevada knew, had been in the back of her mind for a long time.

Because it was as painful as if a dagger had been stuck in her breast, she rose to her feet and went into the Sitting-Room to await Tyrone Strome's arrival.

He came in a few seconds later and she saw that in his hand he held a letter.

She looked at it in surprise and he explained:

"I heard that a Courier was looking for me so I saved him the trouble of coming here."

"You mean people know that this is where you live?"

"Only the people I wish to know it," he answered, "but perhaps I should explain that this letter is of diplomatic importance."

She was curious, but when he put the letter on his desk without opening it she did not like to ask him any more.

"I have neglected my work this morning," he said, as she stood watching him, and she realised he was expecting her to leave him alone.

"It was unlike you to go out riding after break-fast."

"If you are taking me to task," he said with an amused smile, "I must point out that I have only missed a little over an hour's work."

"I was not complaining," Nevada answered quick-ly, "I was only thinking how unusual it was."

"We are keeping almost office hours," he said, "and I am beginning to think it is a mistake. It is cooler today. Would you like to come riding with me?"

"Could I do that?" Nevada asked.

"I have not taken you before for obvious rea-sons," he answered. "But my friends who have been reconnoitering on the outskirts of the town tell me there is no sign of the Sheik's men and I think frankly he will have given up the chase."

"I hope so," Nevada said fervently. "I can really come riding?"

"I am afraid you will have to wear your *litham*," Tyrone Strome said. "But I have a young horse that I think you will appreciate and it can carry a saddle on which you can be comparatively comfortable, even though it does not boast a pummel."

"I will be ready in two minutes."

She ran back to her bed-room to find her *haik*.

She was wearing a new caftan of white silk em-broidered in silver.

It was not, she thought, a very appropriate gar-ment in which to go riding, but there was no time to change.

She put her *litham* over her nose, covered herself with the all-enveloping *haik*, and hurried back to Ty-rone Strome.

"You have been very quick!" he smiled.

"I was afraid you would not wait for me," she replied.

"We cannot go far, you realise that," he said, "because it will soon be too hot, but tomorrow we will start earlier. If you like you can come with me before breakfast."

"I would like that above all things," she replied almost breathlessly.

Tyrone Strome turned towards the door and as he did so a servant came hurrying into the room.

He salaamed but it was obvious that he was agitated and he started to talk very quickly in a high-pitched, excited voice.

Nevada listened but she could not understand what was being said.

She was trying to learn a little of the language by making her maid repeat the name of every object in her bed-room, and she could now say a few sentences such as: "Thank you very much," "May I have some more?" and "Good-night."

Whatever the servant had to report, he was extremely verbose about it, and she realised that Tyrone Strome was listening intently with a serious expression on his face.

Finally the man ceased speaking and because she was anxious and felt instinctively that something was wrong Nevada asked quickly:

"What is the matter? What has he told you?"

"There has been an earthquake."

"An earthquake!"

"Yes, at a village called Sakjena. I must go there at once and see if there is anything I can do to help."

"Let me come with you."

The words were spoken almost before Nevada realised she had said them.

He looked at her, she thought, in surprise.

"Please," she begged.

"Very well," he answered, "the horses are wait ing outside."

A few minutes later they were riding away from the valley and out into the bare stony desert.

The horses were moving quickly and Nevada had to raise her voice to ask:

"How far is Sakjena?"

"About four or five miles," Tyrone Strome replied.

"Surely it is unusual for there to be an earthquake?"

"They happen frequently in this part of the world," he explained, "but they often pass unnoticed when nobody is injured."

There were a hundred things Nevada wanted to ask, but it was difficult to talk at the speed they were riding and she also had to concentrate on keeping herself on her horse's back.

It was quite hard to ride sidesaddle without a pummel, and although the saddle, built something like a child's high-chair, afforded her some support, a great deal of horsemanship was also necessary.

They rode on and now they were back in the country of bare rocky heights of harsh mountain canyons and arid valleys, interspersed with a dry wasteland strewn with boulders.

Then emerging from a defile they saw ahead of them houses built against the side of a high rocky cliff and Tyrone Strome shouted:

"Sakjena!"

There was a thick pall of dust hanging above the place and only as they drew nearer was Nevada able to see that what in the distance had appeared to be houses were now nothing but a huge broken, scattered pile of meaningless rubble.

There were pieces of roofs as well as walls and doors lying in scattered confusion, rocks fallen from the heights above were balanced at strange angles, and moving amongst the whole untidy mess were the figures of men and women screaming aloud in despair or calling out the names of those who were lost.

The noise was ear-shattering and as they rode right up to what had once been a village they could distinguish patches of colour from torn clothing, a

brass bowl glittering in the sunshine, and small house-
hold treasures broken and dusty.

But the full horror of the disaster became apparent when they saw lifeless bodies lying out-
stretched among the debris.

As Tyrone Strome swung himself down from the
saddle of his horse, Nevada noticed a man climbing
over the broken ground towards them and per-
ceived with surprise that he was in European dress.

It was as he reached them that she saw round his
neck he wore a white clerical collar with a patch of
black cloth beneath it.

Tyrone Strome had been giving his horse into the
charge of a young boy, instructing him where to take
it, then as he turned round he exclaimed:

"Reverend! By all that's marvellous! I did not
expect to find you here!"

"Nor I you, Mr. Strome."

They spoke in English, the clergyman with a
strong Scottish accent.

"I came as soon as I heard of the disaster," Tyrone Strome said. "Are there many people buried?"

"Quite a number."

"We shall have to do something about it."

As he spoke he lifted Nevada down from her
horse and another Arab boy took the bridle to lead
it into the shade of some palm trees.

"Nevada, let me introduce the Reverend Andrew Frazer," Tyrone Strome said. "He is a talented doctor as well as a much-respected missionary."

"You flatter me, Mr. Strome!"

The clergyman shook Nevada's hand and did
not seem at all surprised at her appearance.

"Miss Van Arden is an American visitor to Morocco," Tyrone Strome explained. "Find a place to set
up your hospital, and she will help you."

As he spoke a woman came towards them carrying a little boy in her arms.

She was covered in dirt and dust and was wailing
loudly. The child, who appeared to be either uncon-

scious or dead, was bleeding from a cut on the forehead and blood was also pouring from a place on one leg where the skin had been torn away.

Tyrone Strome moved forward, and, as the woman seemed almost incapable of holding the child, he took it from her.

He looked down at the boy for a moment; then holding him out towards Nevada he said:

"He is still alive! The mother will be quite useless in attending to him. Go with Mr. Frazer. He will tell you what to do."

Almost automatically, too surprised to say anything, Nevada took the child in her arms, pushing back the enveloping *haik* to do so.

"Please come with me, Miss Van Arden," Andrew Frazer said.

Tyrone Strome had already walked away and there was nothing she could do but obey.

For the next few hours Nevada had no time to think of anything but the children who were brought to her one after another.

If they were too damaged for her to bandage them and their wounds required stitching, she took them to Andrew Frazer.

But he had his hands full with the men and women who seemed to have suffered more serious injuries in the earthquake than the children.

With an efficiency which came from previous experience, the clergyman had found a portion of a house where he could attend to his patients.

There was part of the roof left to protect them from the sun, and the remains of a back room in what had once been a fairly prosperous house was allotted to Nevada for the children.

A dozen of them were lying on the floor, one or two on mattresses that had been salvaged from the rubble, the rest with nothing better than a cloak or a pile of palm-leaves to keep them from the dust.

The dust was worse than anything else, Nevada thought. It got into her eyes and throat and had seeped into the wounds of the children, so it was difficult to get them clean before she bandaged them.

The noise of their crying because they were frightened and in pain was not so deafening as the row made by their parents wailing for the loss of their possessions and what they feared was the death of their relatives.

Nevada thought it would be easy to persuade some of the women to help her, but she soon realised that they were so completely demoralised and shocked by the catastrophe that they were useless.

Their tears and hysterics made the children even more upset, so with Andrew Frazer's help, who spoke to them in their own language, they were told to stay outside the improvised hospital.

Mercifully after a time they grew tired of making so much noise, or the dust choked them, and they relapsed into a sniffling silence.

When Nevada had time to think of him she knew that Tyrone Strome was working at getting out the bodies that had been crushed by the collapse of the houses and the fall of rocks from the granite cliff against which they had been built.

There was an increasing number of those who were past help laid out in the shadow of the palm trees and covered with any piece of cloth that came to hand.

But there were also quite a number who, though unconscious, could by the skill of Andrew Frazer be resuscitated.

It grew hotter and hotter as midday passed, but the men who were working under Tyrone Strome's orders to excavate those who were still buried laboured on.

Nevada could not help thinking that they might easily have lapsed into inactivity had not Tyrone Strome kept driving them to make further efforts.

Late in the afternoon there was still no help from other places in the vicinity.

"I have sent someone to Tiznet with a long list of my requirements," Mr. Frazer told Nevada when she asked him for more bandages. "I only had the small amount of medical supplies which I always carry, but it is not enough for a disaster such as this."

"The children I bandaged earlier need their dressings changed," Nevada said.

The Scotsman smiled at her.

"I am afraid they'll have to wait, Lassie, but you've done well. You must be awfully tired."

"I am very thirsty," Nevada admitted.

He gave her a drink of water from a goat-skin which tasted even more brackish than the water she had drunk first at the oasis.

"I daresay Mr. Strome will find you something to eat later," he said.

"I am not hungry," Nevada answered. "I only wish there was more I could do. When you have a moment I would like you to see if I have made the bandages too tight. I am afraid I am not very experienced at this sort of thing."

"You've done fine," Andrew Frazer replied, and she smiled at him, thinking she could not have had a nicer compliment.

A small boy came running up to them to say something in a breathless voice.

"What is it?" Nevada asked.

"Mr. Strome has sent a message to say that they have discovered another dozen people. Several are dead, but the rest will be brought to us in a few minutes."

"What can we do without bandages?" Nevada asked.

Then she had an idea.

"My *haik* is rather thick, but at least it is fairly clean. We could tear it into strips."

"That's a good idea, Miss Van Arden," Andrew Frazer replied, "but I think you will find it easier if you use scissors."

He handed her a pair and Nevada sat down on the dusty ground and started cutting.

❋   ❋   ❋

The sun was sinking in a blaze of glory when Tyrone Strome came from the pile of rubble and stones to walk slowly and wearily to where the wounded were being tended.

The clergyman was just covering the face of an elderly man who had died despite his efforts to keep him alive.

As he rose to his feet Tyrone Strome said:

"I do not think we will find any more, and if there are any poor devils left they will be dead by now."

As he spoke he wiped his forehead with the back of his hand, leaving streaks in the grey dust which covered his whole face.

He looked tired, and Andrew Frazer, knowing he was thirsty, held out the goat-skin to him, saying:

"I don't know what we'd have done without you, Mr. Strome."

"I think the people of Sakjena were fortunate we were both here," Tyrone Strome answered.

He glanced down at the wounded lying on the floor and added:

"Most of the injured would certainly have died without you."

"Aye, it was lucky I was in the neighbourhood," the Scotsman said. "'Twas God's guidance that brought me here."

"I will say 'Amen' to that," Tyrone Strome said with a twinkle in his eye. "Have you let them know in Tiznet what you require?"

"Aye, there'll be enough and to spare by the morning. You get home while there is still enough light to find the way. I can manage now, thanks to Miss Van Arden."

Tyrone Strome looked round.

"Where is she?"

"She's with the children, and she's done fine—really fine. I don't know where I would have been without her."

Tyrone Strome walked to the back of the ruined house.

On the floor lying beside the children were a number of their mothers who had calmed down sufficiently to be allowed to stay with them.

At the far end of what had once been a room Tyrone Strome found Nevada.

She was lying on the bare floor with her head on what appeared to be a bundle of rags.

Her once-white caftan was covered in dust and dirt interspersed with smears of blood.

In her left arm cuddled against her breast was a small baby with its head bandaged, and her other hand rested on the shoulders of a little girl of about six who was snuggled close against her.

They were all three asleep, and Tyrone Strome looking down at them saw that the dust on Nevada's face was streaked with tear-stains, and yet at the same time there was a faint smile on her lips.

He looked at her for some time. Then taking the baby from her arms he laid it carefully down, still sleeping, on a mattress beside another child who was also asleep.

As he tried to move the little girl Nevada awoke.

"What . . . is it?" she asked.

"There is no more you can do," Tyrone Strome replied, "I am taking you home."

"I . . . fell . . . asleep."

"It is not surprising," he answered. "You have worked very hard and you must be extremely hungry."

She smiled at him a little vaguely as if she was not quite sure what he was saying. He lifted the little girl from her side and put her down gently with her cheek on the bundle against which Nevada had been lying.

The child never even stirred.

Nevada was standing waiting for him and he put an arm round her shoulders to lead her to where Andrew Frazer was waiting for them.

"I will be over again in the morning," Tyrone Strome said, "and both Miss Van Arden and myself would like to give something towards the restoration of the village. Will you convey that information to whom it most concerns?"

"I'm always thanking you for something, Mr. Strome," Andrew Frazer replied, "so I've no more words left, but you know I'm grateful."

"It is really in the nature of a thanks-offering," Tyrone Strome smiled. "Miss Van Arden and I escaped from a different sort of danger a short while ago and this is the best way we can express our gratitude."

"You know I'll not refuse anything you have to give," the clergyman replied. "Take the Lassie home, she's earned her rest."

Tyrone Strome, with his arm round Nevada, realised she was almost too sleepy to know what was happening.

The horses were still in the charge of the boys. Tyrone Strome spoke to the eldest of them and learnt that he could ride.

The second boy was rewarded with a coin that left him ecstatic with delight. Then holding Nevada in his arms on the front of his saddle as he had done when they rode ahead of the caravan, Tyrone Strome set off towards Tafraout.

It was dark before they got there but the stars were gradually shining brilliant in the sky and he knew the way.

The lights of Tafraout were a guide for the last two miles and only as they rode up to the very door of the Kasbah did Nevada open her eyes and realise she had slept the whole time they were riding home.

She knew again that sense of protection and security that Tyrone Strome had given her when she had been afraid of being overtaken by the Sheik's horsemen.

"How could I have slept when I was in his arms and my head was on his shoulder?" she asked herself.

She had longed for him to hold her closely against

him again, and now she could almost have wept with vexation to think that it had happened and she had not been aware of it.

She heard the shouts of welcome as the servants from the Kasbah greeted them and she knew it was their noise which had awakened her.

Tyrone Strome rode in through the gate and a moment later they had reached the inner door which led to his house.

"We are . . . home!" she murmured.

"Yes, home," he answered.

He steadied her on the saddle as he dismounted, then when he lifted her down he carried her into the house and through the Sitting-Room into her own bed-room.

"You are not to go to sleep again until you have had something to eat," he ordered, "but I expect you would like to wash first."

Having set her down on the side of the bed, he went from the room and a maid came hurrying in with hot water and clean towels.

Wearily, feeling every movement was a super-human effort, Nevada got to her feet and as she did caught a glimpse of herself in the mirror and gave an exclamation of horror!

The only thing that could have brought her back to wakefulness was the sight of herself with her grey dusty face and her hair tied back with a rag which she had found blowing in the wind.

Her gown was so stained and dirty as to be un-recognizable.

It was nearly an hour later before she joined Tyrone Strome in the court-yard with her hair still wet because she had washed the dust from it. The caftan she now wore bore no relation to the filthy blood-stained garment she had told the maid to throw away.

He rose as she came towards him and without speaking put a glass of wine into her hand.

"If I drink this without eating I shall be drunk," she said.

"Never mind," he answered, "if you are, I will carry you to bed."

She laughed and there was a little flush on her cheeks as she sipped the wine.

Then almost immediately dinner was brought to them and as she ate Nevada felt her fatigue slipping away from her. Though she was tired, she was no longer exhausted to the point of collapse.

They both ate almost in silence, and only when the servants had withdrawn did Tyrone Strome say:

"You must go to bed, but before you do so I wish to tell you how wonderful you were."

There was a note in his voice that made Nevada look at him in surprise. Then when her eyes met his, she felt shy and looked away.

"I was . . . frightened," she said, "very frightened of doing the . . . wrong thing, and yet Mr. Frazer was pleased with me."

"Very pleased," Tyrone Strome said. "He said he could not have done without you."

"Nor you! It was you who saved all those people. If you had not been there they would just have gone on wailing and doing nothing."

"Primitive people are the same all over the world," Tyrone Strome said. "They need leadership. When they have that they behave magnificently."

"And that is what you gave them," Nevada said quietly.

"I dug the people out, but the children might have died if you had not tended to them."

"They were so pathetic, and some of the tiny ones were very brave," Nevada said.

Tears came into her eyes as she spoke and she supposed it was because she was so tired. One child had died in her arms and she thought she would never forget it.

She blinked away her tears and felt embarrassed because she knew that Tyrone Strome had seen them.

He was watching her and because she knew his eyes were on her face she looked down at her hands, finding in surprise that her nails were broken and the skin on her fingers was rough in a way it had never been before.

"You must go to sleep," Tyrone Strome said. "We will talk about everything tomorrow."

"Everything?" she asked enquiringly.

"About you," he answered.

She looked at him in astonishment. Then something in the expression in his eyes made her heart beat violently like the drums of the musicians who played for the dancers.

Then she remembered the movements of the dancer in the *Guedra* and felt as if an icy hand checked the thumping of her heart.

Tyrone Strome might wish to talk to her, but whatever he had to say was not what she wanted to hear.

She knew only too well how much he despised her and where his own interests lay.

She could see, almost as if it were happening in front of her, the serpent-like movements of the dancer's arms quivering, the shaking of her whole body, her half-closed eyes, her parted lips, and her long black hair falling over her naked breasts.

Because the vision of the dance moved before her like a mirage she forced herself to rise to her feet.

"You are right," she said in what she hoped was a normal voice, "I am very . . . tired. Good-night."

He too had risen and when she would have moved away he took her hand in his and raised it to his lips.

"Sleep well, Nevada," he said, "and thank you with all my heart."

Chapter Seven

Nevada awoke and realised that it was hot in her room and therefore it must be later in the day than she had expected.

There was also the brilliant golden sunshine coming between the curtains of her window and no wind to billow them out as was usual early in the morning.

She turned over, realising she had slept deep and dreamlessly for a very long time. Then she looked at the clock by her bed and gave an exclamation of surprise.

It was after twelve o'clock!

Sitting up in bed, she rang a little silver bell and instantly her maid appeared.

"Late, very late!" Nevada said, pointing to the clock.

"Master say you sleep," the maid replied in her own language.

Nevada understood what she was trying to convey; at the same time, she felt annoyed that she had not been awakened.

This meant that Tyrone Strome would have gone to Sakjena without her and she wanted so much to be with him and see if there was anything more she could do to help the stricken villagers.

Her maid had left the room and returned with breakfast on a tray.

Nevada sat up in bed to eat it, at the same

time resenting the fact that she had not breakfasted
with Tyrone Strome as they had done every morning
since she came to the Kasbah.

At first she had been too busy telling herself she
hated him to realise what an interesting meal breakfast could be when one was alone with a man.

Then gradually the beauty of the court-yard, the
cool breeze that came in the morning from the high
mountains, the scent of the flowers, and the chirp of
the little Moroccan birds all combined to make their
breakfast a meal which she felt had an attraction all
its own.

Yet this morning, after all that had happened yesterday, when she had a thousand questions to ask and
there was so much she wanted to know, he had eaten
without her and ridden to Sakjena alone.

At the same time, she was honest enough to admit that she still felt tired.

Yesterday had been a long day and it had also
disturbed her emotionally.

She could still feel that moment of horror when
she realised that the child she was bandaging was
dying and there was nothing she could do to keep it
alive.

As its eyes closed and it gasped its last breath
she had carried it to Andrew Frazer.

He had taken it from her, examined the deep
wound on its forehead, which must have been caused
by a falling rock, and then said quietly:

"There's nothing you can do, Lassie, the wee
bairn's gone to God."

As he spoke he had turned away and carried the
little body outside to lay it beside the others awaiting
burial, while Nevada had gone back to the living
children with tears running down her cheeks.

It seemed foolish to mind the loss of one life
when so many people had died in the earthquake, but
she had felt in some way as if she were responsible,
as if there were something more she could have done,
and yet she did not know what it was.

Now with her breakfast finished Nevada lay back

and made a sign to the maid to pull the curtains back over the window.

The sun came flooding in, bringing with it the rising heat, but Nevada was only concerned with the beauty of the pink granite cliffs beneath the clear blue sky.

"A little Eden," Tyrone Strome had called the valley, and that was what it was, Nevada was sure, to him and to everybody else who lived there. But she really had no place in it.

Last night he had said: "We will talk about you."

She had wondered at the time what he meant; now she was certain that what he was going to tell her was that she could go home.

She did not know why she was so sure of this; she just felt that, like the end of a chapter, or perhaps the end of his book, their association or whatever it was had reached a full stop.

Perhaps he was tired of punishing her, perhaps she no longer interested him, perhaps he wanted to be alone as he usually was when he came to his pink Kasbah.

Whatever the reason, Nevada knew that while she longed to see him she was dreading his return.

Because her thoughts worried her and because she was more tired than she realized, she must have fallen asleep again, and when she awoke she found to her astonishment that the heat of the day had passed and it was late in the afternoon.

She rang the bell by her bed-side fiercely, and when the maid came she got up hastily, washing and dressing herself in record time because she was afraid that Tyrone Strome would return and find her indolent.

But when she went from her bed-room into the Sitting-Room there was no sign of him and she walked to his desk to look down at the pages of his book, on which he had not worked for two days.

'Perhaps it is finished,' she thought, and knew that if it was she could no longer be of use to him.

Because she wanted to touch what belonged to

him, her fingers wandered over the pen he used when he was writing, the blotter that was made of red leather like the boots he wore, the pen-tray, paper-weight, and various other small objects which cluttered his desk.

She felt that each one of them had a personal significance for him, and because they belonged to him she felt they loved him and he loved them.

Then, feeling restless, she wandered into the court-yard.

She walked to the fountain, and felt that it was speaking to her with the tinkling fall of its water into the stone basin.

She remembered how she had scoffed at the whole place for being romantic, and yet now she knew that to her it was the most enchanted place in the whole world.

"A place for lovers," she told herself, and felt the colour rise in her cheeks at the thought.

How often had she laughed and sneered at peo-ple who were in love! How often had she jeered at men as she had at David when they told her they loved her and asked her to marry them!

"How could I know that they felt like this?" she asked herself.

She had thought of love as being soft and senti-mental, but what she felt was a pain and an agony which seemed to increase hour by hour, day by day, until it was almost unbearable.

"How can I endure it?" she asked, and knew that when she could not see Tyrone Strome, when he was no longer in her life, it would be even worse than it was at the moment.

Because her whole body was tense, her ears lis-tening for his return and her whole being crying out for him, she walked back to the Sitting-Room to stand at the window looking out onto the valley.

Now the pink cliffs were flecked with gold and the shadows from the sinking sun were as purple as the amethysts that lay hidden in the mountains.

"It is the most beautiful place in the world," Nevada told herself, "and if I leave it I may never be able to come back again."

It was obvious that no-one but Tyrone Strome could bring her through the dangerous stony waste-land.

He had special privileges, while other Europeans, with the apparent exception of the Reverend Andrew Frazer, were excluded from this part of Morocco.

The sun sank a little lower, gilding the tops of the Kasbahs and enveloping the whole valley in a golden rosy radiance which was indescribable.

Then Nevada saw him, saw Tyrone Strome coming towards her as she had seen him the day she realised that she loved him.

Now there was no doubt in her mind of the light round him, a light that came not only from the sun but from the aura he carried within himself.

He was riding quickly as if he was in a hurry to be home, and because she was shy she turned from the window and crossed the room to sit down on the couch to await his arrival.

She heard his voice outside speaking to the servants, then he came in and for a moment because her heart turned a double somersault it was impossible to speak.

She could only look at him, her green eyes seeming to fill her whole face.

"You are rested?"

He smiled at her and walked across the room to put something he carried in his hand down onto the desk.

"I would have liked to . . . go with you."

Even as she spoke Nevada felt it was a mistake to sound reproachful, and yet the hurt that he had gone alone was almost like a wound.

"You were very tired," he said, "and there was nothing more you could do."

"You are sure of that?"

"Quite sure. Andrew Frazer had buried the

dead at dawn, supplies of food and bandages have arrived from Tiznet, and the worst of the wounded have been taken back to the town."

"And . . . the children?"

Nevada asked the question anxiously.

"Most of the children seem to have made a miraculous recovery and the majority are now with their parents. There were five orphans for whom I had to find a home. The *Caid* in Tiznet agreed to look after them."

Tyrone Strome walked towards Nevada as he spoke and sat down on the couch beside her.

A servant appeared with a cup of mint tea and he sipped it before he said:

"I promised that a certain sum of money would be set aside to provide for them. I do not know whether you would like to join me in this."

"But of course!" Nevada said quickly. "You know I would want to do that."

"I felt you would," he answered, "and actually not a very large sum is required. American dollars and English pounds have a high value when translated into Moroccan currency."

"You must be aware that I am not concerned with what it costs in terms of money," Nevada said.

"No, I knew that," he answered.

A servant came in to take away his empty cup and ask him if he required anything else.

He shook his head and once again he and Nevada were alone.

He rose to his feet and walked to the window to look out onto the valley.

"I brought Mr. Frazer back with me," he said.

"Is he staying here?" Nevada enquired.

"No. The *Caid* in the town is his friend. He saved his son's life. He intends to persuade him to lend the people of Sakjena architects to redesign their village. The Tafraoutis have a skill in building that is unsurpassed anywhere in Southern Morocco."

"I could help towards that," Nevada said.

"I thought you would want to. If you remember, I told him so yesterday."

"Yes, of course you did."

There was silence. Then she said tentatively:

"It will be interesting to see what sort of village the Tafraoutis will design outside their own valley. I realise the soil is different and of course the colour."

"I agree with you it should be very interesting," Tyrone Strome said. "Perhaps one day, when it is finished, you will be able to come back and see it."

Nevada was very still.

Then with his back to her Tyrone Strome went on:

"I said last night that we should talk about you. Perhaps this is as good a time as any."

"What do you want to . . . say?"

"What I am sure you want to hear—that you can go home."

Nevada drew in her breath. Then, with an effort, her voice sounding strange, she asked:

"Why have you . . . decided to let me do . . . that?"

He turned round to walk across the room and sit down on the couch beside her.

"Shall I say the lesson, or rather the punishment if you prefer, is over. You have passed your final examination with flying colours!"

"You . . . mean that?"

"After yesterday I should be ungrateful and very unjust if I did not grant you your freedom."

Nevada said nothing and Tyrone Strome went on:

"You asked me why I played God where you are concerned. It was a good question and one that deserves an answer."

He looked at her enquiringly as he spoke, as if he expected her to speak. When she remained silent he said:

"Are you no longer interested?"

"Yes . . . yes, of course."

"I think the answer is that, despite the fact that

you made me angry, I knew instinctively that you were worth saving from yourself."

"You think that is . . . what you have done?"

There was just a touch of defiance in Nevada's voice.

"When I saw the tears on your face yesterday," he said gently, "when I saw you asleep with those children in your arms, I knew, however much you may deny it, that you are a woman!"

"It seems wrong somehow," Nevada murmured, "that it should take an earthquake to prove your point."

"If it had not been an earthquake it would have been something else," Tyrone Strome replied. "The gold was there but I had to dig rather deep for it."

Nevada got to her feet to walk as he had done across the room to the open window.

"And now you are . . . sending me back," she said, "to what sort of life and what sort of existence?"

"The life you knew before," he answered, "but I think you will look at it with new eyes and the impact people will make on you will be different."

"And you think that is what I . . . want?"

She did not turn round but she felt that he shrugged his shoulders and after a moment he said:

"You will still be a great social success, but I think, Nevada, you will be a little kinder to the young men who love you and who are helplessly captivated by your green eyes and red hair."

"And if I am not . . . captivated by . . . them?"

The words were hard to say, but she managed to utter them.

"What do you want of life, Nevada? What are you seeking?"

His voice seemed almost to ring out in the quietness of the room.

It was a question, Nevada thought, that she had asked herself and knew the answer only too well, but that was something she could never tell him.

"What do you want?" Tyrone Strome asked again.

"I . . . I want to . . . stay here," she answered, "here in Morocco. Perhaps I could . . . work with Mr. Frazer . . . perhaps I could build an orphanage for children like the ones who have to be found a home."

She heard her voice speaking hesitantly, then the surprised note in Tyrone Strome's as he asked:

"Do you understand what you are saying?"

"Yes, of course I do! I know now that that is what I want, I cannot . . . go back . . . I have no . . . wish to do so . . . there is nothing for me if I do."

"What do you mean by that?"

She turned round.

He was looking at her and she thought his face was stern and that he had every intention of refusing her request.

She knew he could make it difficult, if not impossible, for her to remain in Morocco, and because she felt she must convince him of her sincerity she said in a voice that trembled:

"H-how can I make you . . . understand? I k-know only too well what you think of me . . . but I have ch-changed. I swear to you that I have changed . . . this is not a whim . . . this is not, as I feel you are thinking, a rich woman's desire for a new play-thing. It is something that matters more to me than anything else has ever done."

"Can you really have changed so much overnight?" Tyrone Strome asked.

"Perhaps it is not entirely a change," Nevada replied, "but just that in the past there seemed to be no possibility of doing anything except what I was brought up to do, to entertain and be entertained, to spend my money on myself."

She felt he was still unconvinced and she said:

"I will . . . tell you something and perhaps it will make you understand why I am as I am."

She looked towards him pleadingly and after a moment he said quietly:

"I am listening."

"I am not making . . . excuses for myself. I am only telling you. Nobody else would understand . . . and perhaps you will not either."

"I will try," Tyrone Strome said.

"My mother died when I was eight years old," Nevada began, "and because I had been with her so much I think it made a bigger impact on me than if I had spent most of my time with Nannies and children of my own age. I could not believe I had lost her."

She did not say any more, but there was a pathetic, tragic sound to her words which told Tyrone Strome that she had suffered as a child suffers from sheer bewilderment at the death of someone they love.

"Having lost my mother," Nevada went on, "I transferred my affection to my father. I loved him and I wanted desperately for him to love me. I used to count the hours until he came home in the evening and try to spend every moment that he was in the house with him."

She turned away to look out over the valley for a moment before she said:

"One evening I was running into the Study to welcome him home and tell him how much I had missed him, when I heard him say to one of the servants:

'Bring me a drink and for God's sake keep that child out of my hair. I have not got time for her.'"

Even as Nevada spoke Tyrone Strome knew that never before had she told anyone what she had overheard, and he realised from the expression on her face what a shock it had been.

"I c-cried when my mother died," Nevada said in a tight little voice, "but when I lost my father I did not cry. I only felt as if I was all alone in a world that was completely hostile towards me."

There was a pause, until with an effort she went on:

"I . . . I suppose my father had some sense of . . . responsibility because shortly after this my Nanny was sent away and I was provided with a young governess."

Nevada gave a little laugh with no humour in it.

"She was everything that I admired and thought attractive. There was something dashing and modern about her that I had certainly not found in my old Nanny. So you will not be surprised that I concentrated all my love on her."

"Were there no other children in your life?" Tyrone Strome asked.

Nevada shook her head.

"Not so that I could make close friends with them. I was a multi-millionaire's daughter, remember, and as such in a class of my own."

She spoke scathingly, then went on:

"Of course I went to parties, but I felt very out of it, despite the fact that the grown-ups gushed at me and the children eyed me with suspicion."

She gave a little sigh.

"They never had to suffer as I had, from going everywhere with a detective behind me in case I was kidnapped, having armed guards patrolling the house and grounds at night, having everyone who wanted to meet me vetted before they were admitted to my presence."

"Was it really as bad as that?" Tyrone Strome asked.

"Worse . . . much worse than I can ever tell you," Nevada answered. "I knew I was not an ordinary child and that I was in fact . . . extraordinary . . . but it took me some time to understand the barriers that separated me from other children of my age."

"But you had your nice Governess."

"Yes . . . I had Beryl Saunders," Nevada said, and something in the way she spoke made Tryone Strome ask:

"What was wrong with her?"

"Need you ask?" Nevada replied. "She found me as much of a bore as my father had done! I can see now all too clearly how tiresome I must have been with my . . . adoration, my fits of . . . jealousy, my insistence that she must be at my beck and call all day and every day."

"Did she get married?" Tyrone Strome enquired.

"I think that would have been easier to bear," Nevada answered. "No. I merely read a letter she was writing."

She gave another little laugh which again had no humour in it.

"It was a very good object lesson in teaching me not to read other people's letters."

"What had she written?"

"She left the letter in the blotter. She had been writing it while I was doing my lessons and when we came back to the School-Room after luncheon she stopped behind to talk to my father's secretary, who was a friend of hers. They were always gossiping together and I was madly jealous because I thought she liked the secretary more than she liked me."

"So you read her letter?"

"I opened the blotter and read it deliberately," Nevada said. "I do not know to this day to whom it was addressed, it may have been to a young man or it may have been to her family. All I know is that one sentence seemed to jump out at me in letters of fire."

"What did it say?"

For a moment Tyrone Strome thought Nevada could hardly bear to tell him, then she replied:

"My beloved Governess, the woman I adored, had written:

'I would not stay in this place for a moment if it were not for the money. If you only knew what I have to put up with, spending my time with a maudlin child who hangs round me like a piece of clinging ivy so that I never have a moment to myself.'"

Nevada drew in her breath as if it was hard to breathe before she went on:

"There was a lot more but I did not bother to read it. I think it was at that moment that I swore I would never again love anybody, never again would I be hurt as first my father, then my Governess, had hurt me."

"I can understand you feeling like that," Tyrone Strome said in his deep voice.

"As I grew older I made up my mind that I would make people suffer as I had suffered," Nevada went on. "I wanted men to fall in love with me so that I could show my superiority to them by knowing I had no feelings except one of indifference towards them and the whole world."

"And now you think you have changed?"

"I suppose everyone has a vulnerable spot, however hard it is to try to shield it."

"And you have found yours?"

"I knew yesterday that I should be happy—at any rate happier than I am at the moment—if I was with children."

"So you have discovered that you have love to give."

"Of course I have love to give!" Nevada retorted almost furiously. "It has been there bottled up inside me all these years, and at least children who are orphans and depend on charity will not be able to refuse it while they are small."

"You think that such a life, looking after other people's children, will make you happy and be enough to satisfy you?"

"Is one ever completely satisfied?" she asked evasively. "At least it will not be the emptiness and the loneliness I have experienced in the past."

There was silence, then pleadingly she said, looking at Tyrone Strome:

"Help me . . . you know I cannot do this without your help."

He rose from the couch and walked towards her. Her eyes searched his face to see if he would accede to what she asked of him.

"You must help me," she said frantically. "If you send me back I shall not know where to start or how to begin, and besides . . ."

She did not finish the sentence and after a moment Tyrone Strome said:

"You are thinking your father might prevent you from doing what you wish to do?"

"I do not think Father cares what I do one way or the other," Nevada replied, "but you know exactly how my friends and acquaintances will behave, what the Press will say! The whole thing will be talked about, written up, and before I know what has happened I shall only be allowed to sit on a Committee, having no direct contact with the children or being allowed to take care of them myself, as I could do here."

"I believe that is more or less true," Tyrone Strome agreed.

"Then . . . you will help me?"

There was an eagerness in Nevada's voice and in her eyes that had not been there before.

He stood close to her, looking down into her face. Then he said quietly:

"I think the answer to your problem is a child, Nevada, but why not one of your own?"

She stared at him in astonishment. Then slowly, very slowly, so that she could hardly believe what was happening, he put his arms round her and drew her close to him.

"Shall I give you a baby?" he asked.

She felt as if the whole world stood still, then his lips came down on hers.

She knew as he kissed her that this was what she had wanted, this was what she had longed for, and this was everything she had dreamt of as her idea of Heaven.

At first his lips were gentle, as if he were afraid to frighten her.

Then as he felt the softness of her mouth beneath his and felt her draw instinctively nearer to him, he held her closer still and his kiss became more demanding, insistent, passionate.

She felt as if they were part of the sunset outside, the pink cliffs, the wonder of the valley, and she felt too as if he drew her very heart from between her lips and made it his.

He raised his head to look down at her shining eyes and trembling mouth and now she could only whisper the words that came irresistibly to her lips:

"I love . . . you! I love . . . you!"

"As I love you," Tyrone Strome answered. "Do you really imagine, my darling, that I would let you look after anyone else's children except mine?"

"I thought you meant to . . . send me away."

"I knew long before I brought you here that you belonged to me and there could be no returning to the life you lived before we met each other."

"B-but you h-hated me, despised me, and were so . . . cruel."

"That was because I knew that you were not really like that inside, my precious. But I did not know then what you had suffered."

He kissed her mouth again and she clung to him until as he felt her quiver in his arms he raised his head again to say:

"You will never be alone or lonely again, that I promise you, and, darling, I need your love."

"Suppose I . . . bore you . . . suppose you find that I . . . love you too much?"

Tyrone Strome smiled.

"You cannot love me too much, and I want not only your love, my darling, but everything else that belongs to you—your eyes . . ."

He kissed them.

"Your glorious flaming hair . . ."

He put out his hand to touch the fiery red tresses as they fell down her back.

"If you only knew how difficult it has been not to touch it and not to kiss you."

He kissed her cheeks, the corners of her mouth, and once again her lips.

"I want to kiss you all over your perfect body, my beautiful one," he said, "and especially your little hennaed feet."

Nevada looked at him with starry eyes, then with

a little murmur she hid her face against his shoulder.

"I love you and I want you to love me," she whispered, "but h-how can I compete with the . . . dancer?"

She felt Tyrone Strome stiffen as if in surprise. Then as she clung to him he put his fingers under her chin and masterfully turned her face up to his.

"The dancer?" he questioned.

Then when she saw the expression on her face he gave a little laugh.

"You are jealous! Oh, my absurd darling, you are jealous and I had not the least idea of it!"

"She was so . . . attractive and I saw the Shiek give . . . her to . . . you."

"Yes, that is what you saw," Tyrone Strome agreed. "But if you knew a little more about this country, my lovely one, you would know that anything you admire in a Moroccan's house is automatically offered to one as a gift."

He kissed Nevada's forehead before he went on:

"The Sheik, as was to be expected, offered me —his honoured guest—the dancer. It was an obligatory courtesy, but it was equally obligatory on my part to refuse such a generous gesture."

"You . . . refused?"

Nevada's eyes were alight, and her lips were trembling and very near to his.

"I refused, darling, because I was already preoccupied with someone else, someone very naughty but irresistible, whom I already loved even though I had fought against acknowledging it."

"I fought against falling in love with you, too," Nevada murmured, "but when I thought of the dancer . . ."

Again she hid her face against Tyrone Strome and he asked gently:

"What did you think about her?"

"I realised I could not . . . compete . . . but I w-wanted to be in your . . . arms . . . I wanted to be . . . close to you . . . for you to love me as I thought you . . . loved her."

"The love that we have for each other, my darling one," Tyrone Strome said, "is very different from what the dancer or any other woman could offer me."

His arms tightened as he said:

"All my life I have been looking for the woman I would love as I love you. Perhaps because I have lived in the East I wanted to capture her, to conquer her, if you like, and make quite sure she was mine and could never belong to anyone else."

"I . . . love you!" Nevada said looking up at him. "I love you . . . completely, with every part of me . . . and I could never, never love anybody else."

"I think to make sure of that I should keep you here," Tyrone Strome said, "and never allow you to see anyone but me or go abroad without a *litham* over your face."

"I would . . . do that . . . if that is what you wanted."

"You mean that?"

"All I want is to be with you. You fill my whole life and there is nothing else but you . . . and you . . . and you!"

His lips smothered the last word and he kissed her with a passion that made them both breathless and the red of the sun seemed to be reflected in Tyrone Strome's eyes when he looked down at her.

"I love you in a thousand different ways," he said, "and although I would like to keep you all to myself there are unfortunately too many things for us to do in the world outside."

"What sort of . . . things?" Nevada asked apprehensively.

"For the moment they seem unimportant beside us and what we feel for each other," Tyrone Strome replied. "But I have in fact been offered a position which I think you would wish me to accept."

"What is it?" she asked.

"The letter which I received yesterday was from the Foreign Office," Tyrone Strome said. "They want me to stay in Morocco for at least a year as an observer of the events that are expected to take place very shortly."

"What events?" Nevada asked in a puzzled tone.

"The British anticipate, although it is not to be talked about, that the French will try to occupy Morocco," Tyrone Strome said. "If this happens, I shall have complete freedom to move about the country because of my special relationship with the Moroccans. The reports which I shall send to Egland will therefore be of diplomatic importance."

"And I can be with you?" Nevada asked.

"Do you think I would accept otherwise?"

"It sounds too perfect, too wonderful, that I can be with you here amongst the people I love already."

She paused, then said excitedly:

"You will teach me to speak the language?"

"There is a great deal I have to teach you," Tyrone Strome said, "and the most important is to love me."

"I love you already, so much that it seems impossible I could love you more."

"I assure you that what you feel now is only the very tip of the ice-berg," Tyrone Strome said with a twist of his lips. "Oh, my precious little love, you are so beautiful, and your red hair tells me there are many undiscovered fires within you that I want to ignite into a blaze that is all for me."

Nevada threw her arms round his neck and pulled his head down to hers.

"Teach me to love you," she begged. "Teach me to love you as you want me to do. I did not know there was a man who could be so magnificent, so marvellous, and so wonderful as you."

She made a sound which was almost a sob as she went on:

"Are you quite sure that this is not a . . . dream and I shall wake up to find we are not in this lovely pink . . . Eden but perhaps dying of thirst in some stony . . . desert?"

Tyrone Strome laughed at the expression on her face, then he picked her up and carried her across the room to the sofa, laying her down on the satin cushions.

He took the ear-rings from her ears so that he could kiss them, then he pulled aside the embroidered caftan to kiss her neck.

"I love you!" he said. "I love you as I have never loved a woman before, and your skin is like the petals of a magnolia."

"Kiss me . . . make me love you!" Nevada said, and now there was a note of passion in her voice that made it deep and not unlike Tyrone Strome's own.

His lips came down on hers fiercely, compellingly, demandingly.

She felt as if he conquered her as he wished to do and made her completely his captive forever.

She was no longer herself but a part of him, ready to be obedient to his slightest wish, even in the air she breathed.

Her body moved against his and she felt the hard touch of his hand through the thin silk of her caftan.

It was so thrilling that the sensation it evoked ran through her veins like fire and rose to her lips so she seemed to be kissing him with flames.

"I love . . . you."

She was not certain if she said the words aloud or they were spoken in her heart.

"God—how much I want you."

Tyrone Strome's voice was hoarse and deep with passion.

Then as she longed for him to hold her closer and still closer he suddenly sat up, releasing her, and she looked up at him with a sudden concern in her eyes.

"What is . . . it? What is . . . wrong?" she asked.

"There is nothing wrong, my adorable one."

"But there is!" she protested. "Why have you stopped kissing me?"

Tyrone Strome smiled down at her.

"We are going out."

"Out?"

"To find the Reverend Andrew Frazer. We are going to be married, my darling, unless you want me to give you a baby without waiting for you to be my wife."

"Can we be married now . . . at once?" Nevada asked.

"It will doubtless be according to the rites of the Church of Scotland," he replied. "But I have a feeling it would be extremely dangerous for you to remain alone here with me tonight."

He was laughing as he spoke.

He pulled Nevada to her feet and she moved close against him, lifting her face up to his as she said:

"I am not afraid of that sort of danger, but I do want to be your wife."

"And that is what I want you to be, my wife now and for all time," Tyrone Strome replied. "Once you are tied to me, my darling, there will be no escape, no going back to the old life."

He was teasing her but Nevada's eyes were very serious as she said:

"I can imagine nothing more perfect than being with you . . . only you."

"And our babies," Tyrone Strome added.

"And there must be lots of them," Nevada cried, "for they must never be alone as I was, unwanted and miserable because no-one wanted my love."

"That is something that will never happen again," Tyrone Strome said. "Get something to cover you and for God's sake put on your *litham!* Otherwise, if you look like that I shall have a dozen Sheiks trying to kidnap you and carry you off to their Harems!"

"I only want to be in your Harem," Nevada said passionately, then she saw the expression in his eyes and added quickly:

"But there will be no-one else there! If you so much as look at another woman I will . . . scratch her eyes out . . . or stab her to death!"

"You may be jealous, my lovely one," Tyrone Strome said, "but I assure you that you are an amateur in that particular emotion compared to me!"

He put his hand under her chin and turned her face up to his.

"Let me make this clear before I marry you. You will behave properly and circumspectly as my wife, otherwise I shall devise a series of even worse punishments than I have already inflicted upon you!"

Nevada laughed and put her lips close to his.

"Am I still a vixen?" she asked softly.

"You are adorable! Fascinating! Irresistible!" he answered. "And very much a woman!"

It was the answer she wanted and she gave a little sigh of happiness.

"Your woman," she murmured, "for all time, and please . . . because I love you so very much and want you . . . desperately, wildly, and very passionately, let us get married quickly."

Then his lips came down on hers and she surrendered herself to the rising fire which consumed them both.

It was part of the beauty of the valley, the pink Kasbahs, the rose-tinted cliffs, the burning sun, the star-strewn sky, and the wind blowing from the desert.

It was deep in the soul of love, divine, yet so mysterious and secret it would take them a lifetime to discover the perfection of it.

"You are mine," Tyrone said masterfully. "Mine so that your thoughts are my thoughts, your heart is my heart, and your body is mine from the hairs on your lovely head to the toes on your little feet."

"I love . . . adore . . . and worship you," Nevada whispered.

Her voice broke on the last words, but they were lost against his lips as he held her completely and utterly captive.

ABOUT THE AUTHOR

BARBARA CARTLAND, the celebrated romantic author, historian, playwright, lecturer, political speaker and television personality has now written over 150 books. Miss Cartland has had a number of historical books published and several biographical ones, including that of her brother, Major Ronald Cartland, who was the first Member of Parliament to be killed in the War. This book had a Foreword by Sir Winston Churchill.

In private life, Barbara Cartland, who is a Dame of the order of St. John of Jerusalem, has fought for better conditions and salaries for Midwives and nurses. As President of the Royal College of Midwives (Hertfordshire Branch), she has been invested with the first Badge of Office ever given in Great Britain, which was subscribed to by the Midwives themselves. She has also championed the cause for old people and founded the first Romany Gypsy Camp in the world.

Barbara Cartland is deeply interested in Vitamin Therapy and is President of the British National Association for Health.